THE BOSS

P J ADAMS

JOHN BLAKE

Published by Blake Publishing Ltd,
3 Bramber Court, 2 Bramber Road, London W14 9PB, England

First published in paperback in Great Britain 2001

ISBN 1 185782 400 8

British Library Cataloguing-in-Production Data:
A catalogue record for this book is available
from the British Library.

Typeset by Jon Davies

Printed and bound in Great Britain by
Creative Print and Design (Wales) Ebbw Vale, Gwent

1 3 5 7 9 10 8 6 4 2

There's no need to hang about waiting for
the Last Judgement — it takes place every day.

Albert Camus, *The Fall* (1956)

INTRODUCTION

My name's Tony Mills. You probably won't have heard of me, but by the time you've finished reading this book you won't ever forget who I am. I was born and bred in Hoxton, right slap bang in the middle of the real East End of London. Old lags are always crapping on about what a tough place it was but I survived by keeping on my toes and never letting anyone take the piss.

I've done a lot of bad things in my life but I never hurt no one who didn't deserve it. When I was a kid I knocked around with some right nutters who'd rob their own grannies as soon as look at them. But I didn't live by their code. I wanted to make it in the real world, not down in the gutter. There it's all just a desperate fucking scramble for survival.

But no matter how hard I tried to make an honest living out in the markets, then in boxing and later the bare knuckle fight game, those leery bastards just kept coming back to haunt me. They built me up as a tasty fighter by calling me "The Boss" inside the ring because that's what I was; the number one scrapper; the smartest hitter in the East End.

Trouble was, those same characters owned me and used me. Maybe I was always doomed to end up in jail, but I never in my life broke a law that really mattered.

Once I was banged up, I had to learn to live by an even tougher code — because that was the only way to survive. I made sure everyone knew me as "The Boss" when I went inside because respect is the only currency screws and inmates deal in. Being a hard man meant I did things inside that I now regret. But they had to be done. I had no choice.

People like me are built to try and beat the system. I never crumble under pressure. I never back down. So I became, in a sense, two people inside prison. One was the big, strong tough guy who struck fear into the inmates and screws.

The other me was a quieter, more thoughtful bloke who only wanted to care for his wife and child, but had that opportunity snatched away by being convicted of a crime he never committed. Now I know that's what all cons say but, as you'll find out later in this story, I really didn't deserve to be put away.

I never knowingly hurt an innocent person but if

anyone crosses my family or friends I will hunt them down and make them pay. That's the way I am; an eye for an eye; a tooth for a fucking tooth.

Revenge. It's a word that can burn away your soul and split your heart in two. No doubt about it.

It turned me into a fighter. It turned me into a convicted killer. It turned me into an impatient man.

Revenge doesn't pay the bills. Revenge doesn't bring you love. Revenge doesn't create a happy family. Revenge just eats up everything in its path.

But it was the driving force behind the story I'm about to tell and because we all feel a measure of it at some time in our lives I think it's worth a spin.

PROLOGUE

HMP Parkhurst, Isle of Wight,
3.00pm, 30 May 1999

Nick the Greek was standing by the door to the prison gym. He was with two other inmates, both white, both with close-cropped hair and both with the sort of thick necks you see on all those dickhead jailhouse studs. Nick nodded to me and Gentle Jack.

"All clear," he said, and motioned us to get to the ring. As prison gym orderly, Nick was the key to what was about to take place.

I gave him the thumbs up.

The only light in the gym was natural light from the six overhead skylights. Every time the sun broke through the clouds outside, long dusty beams of light cut through the greyness.

In the corner of the gym, a temporary ring had been put up. It had unpadded wooden corner posts with metal bases nailed on in the prison workshop. Each pole had two hooks on its inside to thread the ropes through. One rope was red, the other white. They'd been lifted from the prison reconstruction area. There was no matting on the floor. It was going to be a hard fall for anyone hitting the deck.

At least thirty inmates gathered around the ring on two sides. The other sides were up against a wall. They shuffled closer to the ring to make sure that any uninvited guests wouldn't clock what was going down. There was even a bit of an atmosphere brewing between my mob and fans of Gentle Jack Duncan — a man convicted in the outside world of killing three people with his bare hands. Nothing fucking gentle about that.

I spotted a trainer's bucket in the centre of the ring that was stuffed full of phone cards — the only hard currency that matters inside. An inmate in a clean white T-shirt was pulling out handfuls of them and counting them on to a mat.

I stood in my corner and looked across at Gentle Jack. He was completely bald but had a grey goatee beard that made his face look even rounder. He looked pale and flabby. Not very impressive.

He looked over fifty but I'd heard he'd only just hit the big four O. People usually age pretty well in the nick, so fuck knows what had happened to him. He had on smelly-looking grey sweatpants and a pair of filthy white trainers. He walked back and forth between his corner and the centre of the ring like a caged animal.

Then there was me. Tony "The Boss" Mills. I'd already pulled off my training top to show off my broad shoulders and thick chest. I wanted Gentle Jack to see that I was in top condition. But then I had been pumping iron in prison for nearly twelve years.

Gentle Jack's mouth seemed to have developed a twitch when I looked across at him. He was grating his teeth and every now and again his tongue took a swipe across his lips. And his eyes were wide and staring. Looked to me like he'd got hold of some gear. Not such a difficult thing to do in the slammer. I never touched the stuff. It's the Devil's poison.

Our ref for the match was an old cat burglar called Gerry Wright. He came and stood next to me.

"He looks fit, looks good don't he?" Gerry mumbled.

I smiled because nothing could be further from the truth. Gentle Jack looked a right fucking state to me. But then this was no grudge match, no prison yard flare-up. This was a cold-start fight, a real fight with a lot of phone cards riding on it. Another test. Truth was I'd rarely been really tested in all the time I'd been inside.

Then some of the cons started getting a bit lippy.

"Fuckin' 'ammer him, Jack," one yelled. Then they

all started ranting and raving.

"Give him summa that," said another, waving his fist in my direction.

"Keep it down," Gerry shouted. Smart lad. He knew that if we made too much of a row, we'd be rumbled and the contest would be over before it had begun.

Gerry was both referee and judge. Another old lag called Del acted as timekeeper and held a tin plate and spoon to sound the rounds. The fight was set for four two-minute sessions, kicking, butting, gouging, biting and rough-housing was all legit. Gerry's refereeing meant fuck all really.

The crowd went dead quiet. My stomach turned over. I could feel the tension building. I was up for it, all right. Let the battle commence.

The plate clanged. Me and Gentle Jack headed into battle. I swung huge random punches straight at him because I knew I had a longer reach. He walked straight into them like a juggernaut into a brick wall.

Then he kicked out and caught me in the bollocks. I doubled up but managed to step back as he followed through with a flurry of uppercuts. Clumsy bastard completely missed me.

I straightened up and aimed an elbow right across the bridge of his nose. I swear I heard something crack. He put his hands up, his chin down and kept coming at me. Tough bastard.

Then he threw a vicious right hander. This time I didn't see it coming. It flew into the side of my head, just above my ear. Felt like a crowbar smashing into my skull.

"You got 'im, Jack. You fuckin' got 'im," I heard one con shout.

"Go on, Jack, finish the cunt off," screamed another.

I tried to shake the pain out of my head. My legs were like jelly so I backed off and bobbed and weaved for a bit to give me time to recover.

My upper body swung heavily to one side, but my feet somehow stayed firm. I looked up to find a confused look on Gentle Jack's face. He thought he'd got me. Now he'd run out of ideas.

Outside the ring, he was more used to kiddie killers and nonces who stayed down once they'd been whacked. I'd taken his best shot and stood firm. Jack wasn't bright enough to follow through and try to finish me off.

Then he tried to grab me by the arms and fling me to the floor but all the stupid tosser managed to do was lose his balance. I flicked my right foot around his ankle and sent him crashing to the floor. The bell saved him.

Jack took a faceful of cold water from a saucepan provided by a poofy lifer who'd volunteered to be his second. He then stood up defiantly with his arms spread across the flimsy top rope either side of his corner. He was trying to look as if he was ready for the kill.

Meanwhile I was trying to get my act together. Just then a dog-breath smelly voice whispered in my left ear, "Charge him. He'll never see it comin'. He's too fuckin' thick."

I thought I was being set up for a fall so I didn't take

a blind bit of notice.

The tin plate clanged for the second then the third. They were bad times for me. Gentle Jack tore into me. He came at me over and over again like a fucking lunatic on speed. My prison title looked all but lost.

His punches and kicks felt like I was being done over with sledgehammer. The crowd was all quiet. They thought they was watching me die. A flabby, overweight psycho from Dagenham was ripping me apart.

Every punch and kick I took made it harder and harder to stay on my feet. A horrible mistiness filled my head. I could hardly focus on what was happening. Everything seemed to be happening in slow motion. I wasn't even sure I was still in this world. I flung my fists and feet at him with no idea whether I was coming close to hitting the bastard or not.

I could hear myself breathing and snorting with pain each time he scored another direct hit. The violence was relentless. Red rain poured down in front of my eyes.

On the third bell I knew that another half a minute and I was a gonner. Then that same voice whispered in my ear, "I told you to fuckin' charge him. Head down. He'll go down. I promise. He'll go down."

This time I let the words sink in.

I clenched my fists hard and jumped to my feet with a final burst of energy. I looked across and tried to focus on the job at hand. I forced myself to stop blinking, even though there was blood in my eyes. The bell went. I looked straight at him.

He seemed distracted by something and was glancing to the side of me at someone else. Head down I charged straight into him. My head sunk into his chest with an almighty thud.

I kept charging until he smashed up against the ropes that ran alongside the gym wall. His head flew back and cracked against the brickwork.

Gentle Jack's eyes rolled as his head flew forward from the wall. He blinked hard. His head fell to one side. His knees buckled underneath him and he crumpled down on top of himself. I caught him with a knee full in the face as he headed for the floor.

Gerry tried to pull him to his feet but his arms had gone like a rag doll's. Then his head sagged forward again and he doubled up in a heap on the floor.

There wasn't time to raise my hand in victory. I didn't even get a chance to see whether Gentle Jack was alive or dead. Not that I gave a fuck. I had to get out of there before I keeled over myself and I pushed quickly through the crowd. A handful of inmates started dismantling the makeshift ring.

Just before I reached the gym door, I turned to see Gentle Jack being dragged off by four cronies. Other cons who'd put him up for the fight in the hope of hurting me looked incensed. Those who'd bet on him had lost their hard-earned phonecards and a couple of them aimed kicks at the loser.

"Lucky bastard," Gerry the ref grunted at me as we headed through the gym doors and down the corridor towards B wing.

As we moved along the shiny red vinyl floor I pulled on a grey sweatshirt and acknowledged the congratulations of a few inmates with the occasional nod and smile.

But inside I wasn't happy. Once I'd been a fighter with a fearsome reputation and a decent wedge of cash to match. What the fuck was I doing in that sort of battle? I'd been reduced to jailhouse scraps with no rules and phone cards for prize money.

I decided there and then that would be my last fight while I was inside. I had three months left to serve of my sentence and I needed to start thinking about life on the outside after twelve years in that shithole.

Violence had been the key to my survival for too long. I knew I hadn't lost my bottle, but I couldn't keep on taking punishment like that without ending up a basket case. No, I had to make a new start in life. It was now or never.

1

HMP Parkhurst, Isle of Wight,
5.30am, 15 September 1999

I stepped out of the gate, heard it sliding shut behind me, and thought to myself, "Well, mate you're on your tod now. No more nice gentle screws to bring you breakfast, dinner and tea and tuck you up in bed at night."

My old windcheater felt cold after the thick prison uniform. I stopped for a few seconds outside the building, and looked back at the gates.

I shivered. Not from the cold but as my old uncle Billy would say, "because someone just walked over your grave, son." That was the only sign I needed to get the hell out of that place before they changed their minds and dragged me back inside again.

I'd be a liar if I said it felt good to be free again. I was bloody terrified. All I had to my name was the suit I was standing in and a holdall in one hand containing a razor, a clean shirt and some clean underwear — all care of Her Majesty's Prison Service.

I only had £100 cash from my workshop job because I'd sent all the rest to my kid.

That was it. All I owned in the world. I had nowhere to live and there was a good chance I'd be back inside before not too long.

I'd hit middle age. I had a daughter who'd grown up without me, but the strange thing is I didn't really feel old.

One veteran I shared a cell with told me once he reckoned life in the slammer kept him young and healthy. He had a point.

"The outside world moves at a hell of a pace," he said, "while we're all stuck in here frozen in time. No reason to get old if you ain't got the problems they 'ave out there, son."

At the bus stop in front of the prison I passed two screws on their way in to start the day shift. They clocked me, but didn't say a word. If they had I think I'd have banged their fucking heads together. I was that wound up. Tight like a ball of wire.

Soon I was in the bus and on my way to the railway station. I couldn't believe that a two-mile journey cost more than a nicker. Now I had less than 99 quid on me.

At Newport station I handed my rail warrant in at the booking office. The geezer behind the bullet proof glass looked at me over the top of his specs like I was some sort of scum, and handed me a one-way ticket to Waterloo without saying a word.

The train took me to Ryde, where I hopped on a hovercraft across the Solent. As the thing rose off the tarmac I looked out of the steamy porthole and studied the coastline. I hoped that was the last time I'd ever see the Isle of Wight; good fucking riddance. I never wanted to set foot on the bloody place ever again.

The other cons told me it was the air you first noticed when you were out. Air doesn't always have to smell of disinfectant, they said. You think this is normal ... wait 'til you smell real air again.

I didn't take a lot of notice of them at the time, to be honest about it. My mind was always on more pressing matters. But now I was out I remembered every word.

They weren't completely right, though. Air that whiffed of Vim had never smelt normal to me, and the memory of it had disappeared as quickly as the big, sliding steel door shutting behind me that morning.

Dozing on the Portsmouth to Waterloo train, uncomfortable in my old suit, I started thinking about the sounds I'd left behind.

Prisons were bloody noisy places, night and day: doors crashing open and closed, the mesh in the stairwell clattering when anyone moved along the galleries, people bawling all the time, kicking up a racket because everyone — and I mean the screws and the inmates — was bored out their skulls.

The train that day felt dead silent to me in comparison. Twice I wiggled my finger in my earhole just to be sure I was where I thought I was. Maybe trains had got quieter in the last twelve years? But the sandwiches were just as bloody stale.

An hour later I found myself standing in the road just outside Waterloo Station, soaking up the peace and quiet of early morning London.

It was still too early for the main rush-hour but commuters and lorries was already starting to jam up the city streets. And then there was the black cabs. They looked almost the same except some of them weren't black no more. Luckily they still made that same familiar deisel clunking noise; engines, tyres, exhaust ... peace and quiet, London style.

At Waterloo, I got a 49 bus to the Central After Care Association on account of if I hadn't, I would have been banged up again within 24 hours for violating my licence.

I sat in the drab waiting room opposite a couple of old lags puffing away on rollups. It was just like being back in the joint. I'd been the only inmate on my floor who didn't live on cancer sticks. I hated smoking so much. Nicotine is the only drug in life that kills others as well as yourself.

About half an hour later this probation officer comes out of his office and tells me to follow him.

"Well, Tony," says the man. "Welcome back to the

real world. D'you reckon you'll survive?"

Very bloody encouraging, don't you think? I felt like popping the geezer but I buttoned it and went on an all-out charm offensive.

"Hope so," I replied through gritted teeth. No way was I going to call this smarmy git "Sir".

"Now then ... " he went on, turning over the pages of my record on the desk in front of him. "Let me see. You haven't got anywhere to live, is that right?"

"Course, I fuckin' haven't, you wally," (I thought to myself).

"Yeah," I replied.

"Well, we need to sort that out, don't we?"

I hated the way he said "we" as if he was dealing with some thick-headed eight-year-old kid.

"We should book you a room at Ralston House for the night and then you can try and find some digs tomorrow."

Bloody marvellous. When I got banged up for a murder I didn't commit I had a tasty detached five-bed house in Chigwell with all mod cons. Now I was about to call a half-way hostel my only home.

I couldn't wait to bed down at the dosshouse, get a dose of lice and sit around watching old lags scratching their wooden legs and puffing away on dogends.

"I'd like to try for somewhere else," I said.

"Don't see as you've got any choice," he replied.

I didn't answer. I just shrugged my shoulders. I couldn't be fucking bothered with this prat.

"Then, we've got to get you fixed up with a job."

I grunted in agreement.

"What would you like to do?"

What would I like to do? I'd like to get a stretch limo and head down to the Costa Del fucking Sol and lie in the sun with a pina-fucking-colada and a couple of tasty birds on my arm. Was that what he had in mind? Was it bollocks!

"S'ppose I could get a job as a doorman at a club or somethin'," I suggested.

"That'll hardly keep you out of trouble," said the smarmy git.

I glared at him. He swivelled round on his chair and started tapping something out on the desktop computer in front of him. As the printer fired up, he turned back to me.

"Take this to the centre and they'll try and fix you up with something."

He put the letter in an envelope, stuck it down and then handed it to me. I stuffed it in my jacket pocket and got up to leave.

"Good luck," he said for probably the fiftieth time that month. He was grinning and offered me his hand. I ignored it.

"Call me and let me know how you get on."

I didn't say a word, just turned and walked out of his office and out of the front door into the street.

What a waste of bloody time. I headed to a nearby caff and forced myself to put away some bacon and eggs.

Even though I hadn't eaten anything since my last lousy plate of porridge at five that morning, I couldn't get a normal brekky down on account of it being so rich. It'd be a few days before I could handle real food again.

I signed on at the job centre that morning like a good little boy. They didn't have anything for me (surprise, surprise), so I headed back onto the streets.

None of the pedestrians seemed to even notice me but I couldn't stop looking at all of them. Different clothes, different colours, different faces, different buildings, different cars. A different world.

That's when I decided I had to go and see Brenda and our daughter Karen.

You see, soon after getting banged up, my missus Brenda came for a visit to tell me that our marriage was over. She'd wanted to keep it going, but my absence wasn't making her heart grow any fonder. She needed security. She needed a man. I could give her fuck all.

Little Karen was destined to grow up without a dad and we both knew the problems that could lead to. Brenda said she had to think of the future and the way she booked it, that didn't include me.

I understood but I begged her not to divorce me until I got out. I promised I'd keep away from her if she met someone else but I had to have a goal to aim for when I got released, even if it was completely pointless because I'd probably already lost her.

After that final visit by Brenda my brain went awol for a while. I beat some poor bastard to a pulp after a row over a plate of spaghetti in the prison canteen. Unfortunately this geezer's best mate was rated one of the hardest bastards in Parkhurst. I was challenged to a bare-knuckle straightener.

My reputation as "The Boss" was already well known, thanks to the other East End inmates. A couple of blaggers from Dalston pushed me to take on this so-called hard nut. I'd kept fit in the prison gym so I was up for it. It started out a promising scrap, too, but in the end I beat seven shades of shit out of him. And that's how I carried on fighting — and surviving — inside.

But now I was back in the real world and that meant living by a different set of rules.

2

Over to one side, near where the steps lead up to Charing Cross Tube Station just north of the Thames, an old boy in a brown plastic apron was opening up a flower stall. He and a younger lad, who'd just arrived in a van that looked so small you could have picked it up and popped it in the glove box of any decent motor, were unloading tulips and chucking them in plastic.

Last time I'd been past here a legendary blagger called Jerry North had been running the stall. It had filled his days since his retirement. We'd been on nodding terms because he'd been down to see a few of my fights in the old days. Then I heard the silly bastard went and topped himself while I was away. Apparently he just couldn't hack it in the outside world. God rest his soul.

Anyway, I watched this old boy and his sidekick setting up those flowers for a couple of minutes. I tucked my thumbs into my waistband. My old strides felt tight as a duck's arse.

I'd always been a smart dresser. It added to my reputation as "The Boss" in the fight game when I thrashed challengers at the rate of one a month. Back in those days I favoured three-piece whistles with a gold watch and chain, Turnbill and Asser shirts, plus handmade soft black leather shoes.

That morning I was decked out in the same suit I'd been wearing the day I was nicked.

It just about summed up what prison was all about. They took twelve years of my life, and just so I wouldn't notice, at the end of it all they turfed me out in the clothes I'd worn on the way in, as if I wouldn't give a toss. As if nothing had changed.

Some old lags might not have minded, but feeling the tightness of the waistband on my strides really bothered me. Now I'm no lard arse but it reminded me that — even though I was still fit and strong — I was developing a slight middle-aged gut.

On the train I'd tried to get some kip and even loosened the top of my trousers. Then I caught some old grannie looking at me as if I was some kind of nonce about to flash her.

That first day out I felt like a bloody alien from another planet. I needed some new clobber, and I wanted to keep my fitness up. Though maybe not in that order.

But first of all I had to find a way of fitting back into the outside world. It wasn't going to be easy.

I strolled over to the flower stand as the little delivery van pulled off. The old boy was unloading yet more flowers from the buckets into wooden boxes lined with green stuff that was supposed to look pretty.

He finally noticed me standing there, but ignored me.

"Got any daffs?" I asked him.

"Over there."

They were at the far end of the stall, high up at the back. I reached across and took down a bunch. They were still wet, and bound tightly together with elastic bands.

"Four fifty," the old boy said.

I started digging in my pocket before it hit me.

"Four pound fifty?" I asked holding up half a dozen blooms.

He shrugged. I fingered through the coins: some of them were mine from twelve years back, some of them were from the rehabilitation hand-out. Then I passed over the exact money.

"You gonna wrap them for me, then?" I asked.

"If you ask me nicely."

"I just did."

He took the flowers from me and swirled them into a neat cone, tweaking the pointed end into double thickness to make a grip. The water didn't seem to seep through with the paper folded like that.

"Thanks a lot," I said.

But the old boy had already turned away from me. He was back with his flowers, trying to make them look nice enough to lure more mugs like me. There were plenty of us around to keep the likes of him going.

I walked across London that afternoon, partly to save money and also because I thought the exercise would do me good. Wearing that old suit had come as a bit of shock.

I'd always held my weight well. I was proud of my strong, wide frame. I had one of the biggest chest expansions on the East End fight circuit at my peak. I'd never had to watch my weight.

But then that was something to do with the way I always used to live: lots of getting about, lots of activity, most of it legit. That's why sitting on the edge of a narrow bed 20 hours a day didn't exactly come natural to me.

London looked cleaner than I remembered it. But then it was a boom town compared with what it had been when I'd taken my one-way ticket to Parkhurst.

There were a handful of new buildings, and a lot of spruced up old ones. The number of motors on the streets took me by surprise. A lot of them had their number plates lettered a different way round.

And there were loads of foreign cars, or certainly a lot more than I remembered. Looking at all those wheels reminded me that I needed a car myself. I hadn't a clue how I'd manage that.

In the old days motors were never a problem if you

knew the right people. But I wasn't sure if I still did.

I walked up the Embankment, pausing to have a closer look at the river. Even that looked cleaner. I'd never felt sentimental about London. It was just the place I was born and bred. But now for the first time I appreciated the look of it, the feel of it, the smell of it.

I spotted a familiar newsagent's shop just up from the Embankment tube station so I crossed the road and went in.

I counted my money out carefully and bought a box of chocolates, choosing the one with the biggest box but costing the least. The woman behind the counter wanted an extra nicker to wrap it so I settled for a brown paper bag. Story of my life, I guess.

As I strolled on, I got a better feel for my surroundings. Small groups of tourists and kids of all ages and nationalities passed by me.

None of them gave me a second glance but I clocked every single one of them. They looked different from what kids had seemed like before. There was every different skin colour you could imagine yet they was all laughing and joking together. Some things had changed for the better.

I walked for miles, eventually I turning a corner into the street my wife and daughter now called home. I smoothed my hand over my hair. It had been cropped short in the nick, but I liked it that way and intended to keep it.

In any case, it wasn't nearly as out of place as it might have been twelve years back. These days every other geezer out on the streets seemed to have the same cut. I checked the tightness of my tie knot and glanced down at my flies.

I felt okay — all things considered.

Brenda and Karen were living back in Hoxton, in a place they called the Rat Run. It was on one of those rundown overspill estates built on a slab of bomb damaged wasteland in the early sixties. The prettiest thing about it were the redbricks they used to build it.

Daffodils in one hand, chocolates in the other, I walked across the tarmac in front of the building where they lived – Tavistock House. The middle of London might have had a facelift, but somewhere along the line they missed out the council estates of Hoxton.

Brenda's flat — crammed next to about a dozen identical others on the third floor — overlooked a vandalised playground.

Karen had told me in one of her letters that their flat had two bedrooms, a living room, a sliver of a kitchen and a bathroom. The only natural light came through one big, cracked, metal-framed window that overlooked the old Hoxton candle factory.

I caught the rancid smell of burning wax in the air as I walked past the smashed up shell of a Sierra dumped in the car park in front of the Rat Run. I looked up at the row of flats where Brenda lived and hoped she wouldn't see me. I wasn't even sure if I had the bottle to knock on her door. Pretty fucking fearless tough guy, eh?

I had bugger all to offer Brenda other than a dream that things might get back to the way they were.

Karen never said in her letters what Brenda was doing. How she was surviving. If someone special had come into her life.

Now I was about to find out.

I passed an old geezer sitting on a bench rolling up a fag. A little kid played not far from him on the rusty swings in the wrecked playground.

Just then I felt someone sneaking up on me from behind. In the joint I would have faced them up straight off, but I knew it was different on the outside so I carried on walking.

Then there was a tap on my shoulder. I turned and came face to face with some kid — no more than 16 — with a nose filled with green snot and a glazed expression in his eyes.

"Gotta fag?" he asked.

"Nope."

"Go on. You must 'ave one."

"They're bad for you," I told him.

He looked at me liked the glazed junkie he so obviously was.

"N" I paused, "... fucking ... O."

Then he pulled back faster than a cat on a fucking bonfire and ran off towards a row of shitty lock-ups — no doubt after another fix.

Just as he headed across the road a young girl appeared walking towards him. There was something about her that looked familiar. I squinted to try and get a better look.

Was it my own daughter Karen? It definitely looked like her but if I confronted her then Brenda would think I was stalking her.

I watched the ciggie-poncing junkie hand the girl a silver foil wrap. She looked a right mess. Her hair was tied back in a greasy ponytail and her clothes were filthy. Was this really my own kid? My own flesh and blood?

I couldn't just stand by and do nothing so I ran towards them. The moment they saw me approaching they scarpered off towards the underground car park below Brenda's block.

I squeezed between two dirty white Transits and tried to head them off but once I got into the car park it was so dark I lost sight of them. I'd never even got close enough to see if it really was Karen

I walked over to the lift entrance. Graffiti had been sprayed all over the walls. Fuck knows what it all meant. Most of it looked foreign to me. I pressed a chipped red button. It didn't respond and there was no sign of an elevator firing up so I started climbing the concrete stairs. The whole stairwell stank of piss. This place made Parkhurst seem like a perfume factory.

I tried to ignore it all. I had more important things to think about. For the first time in 12 years I was going to try and act like a real father.

I took the steps up to the third floor of Tavistock House two at a time. The door to number 14c was in need of a qood lick of paint, but all that could wait a while. Two rusting dustbins stood by the door, one on each side, like guards.

My finger was shaking as I pressed the doorbell.

What a state to get yourself in. Here I was, the hardest bastard in the East End, scared shitless of meeting my own wife and daughter. At first nothing happened. Then I pressed harder. I could just hear a chime squeaking in the distance.

Flowers still in hand, I nervously wiped back my hair one last time. Just then a noise behind me made me turn.

A small gang of white teenagers in wraparound sunglasses and shell suits was hanging about: one of them was leaning up against the wall at the end of the corridor, while the others were smoking what looked and smelt like a fat reefer.

They were watching me, grinning at each other.

I turned back to the door.

There was some movement behind the frosted glass window. A pale hand reached up to turn the lock.

As the door swung slowly open, I thought I'd come to the wrong house, or maybe I was on the wrong estate. A girl stood there; a stranger to me – fair-skinned, fair-haired, skinny, half girl/half woman.

She stared back at me, seeming to recognise me ... but she was scared.

I smiled. Thank God it wasn't the kid I'd spotted a few minutes earlier buying some smack on the street below.

She said: "You want Mum?"

"Karen?" I said. "Are you ...?"

"Mum!"

She turned back towards the inside of the flat, her skinny hand still holding the dirty brass knob of the lock, an inch or two too high for her.

"Karen ... listen!" I leaned in towards her, and touched my forefinger to my lips. "It's me! Ssh ..."

"What d'you want?"

The last time she'd been just a baby ... four, five, mucky face crying in the prison visitor's area. Suddenly the kid had become a woman. I knew she'd have grown up but not like this ... Beautiful as she was, she looked worn out. There were big black rings under what should have been sparkling blue eyes.

"Who is it, Karen?" came a brittle, familiar voice from inside.

Brenda appeared from the direction of the kitchen, wiping her hands down the front of her apron. Karen glanced back, then at me again. Her expression had changed: the confusion had gone. Now she looked terrified. The door began to close.

As I moved forward the Daffadils fell lose in my hand.

Then Brenda spotted me.

"Get inside, love," she said to my daughter, but Karen stayed frozen to the spot. Brenda elbowed her out of the way.

"Fuck off outta here!" she screamed at me.

The door swung at me but I crashed my boot down and blocked it.

"Just wanna talk," I pleaded.

"No."

"Please, Brenda."

"Karen, inside!"

She now had her full weight on the door, trying to

force it against my foot. Karen stood back in the hallway, her arms hanging limply by her sides, staring at me, staring and staring.

"Mum ...?"

"I said, inside!" yelled Brenda.

"Gissa minute, Brenda. Only a minute. Please."

"She doesn't know you, Tony. She doesn't want to know you!"

The woman I married eased the pressure on the door for a split second and I managed to force it wider open. But then Brenda threw her full weight back against the door, slamming it against my arm and knocking the flowers out of my hands.

I made a grab for them as they fell, snatching at the heads ... and yellow petals sprayed around me, almost in slow motion.

"I only wanted to talk to you," I shouted.

"Talk to me? You want to talk to me? You ain't existed for twelve fuckin' years and now you want to talk to me? Piss off!"

"You can't do this to me!"

"You did it to yourself!"

"I have a right to see my kid."

"Well, she doesn't wanna see you."

Brenda was shaking with rage.

I caught a glimpse of Karen, still frozen in horror, and realised I had to pull out because of the effect all this aggro was having on her.

I took a step back and the door slammed shut.

Brenda's screaming had finished me off: I hated anyone screaming at me. I flung what remained of the battered daffodils at the door. They scattered and fell.

"Only wanted to say hello ..." I bawled at the tatty door as Brenda double locked it. "... that's all ... bloody hello!"

I hurled the brown paper bag containing the chocolates at the door; it missed and bounced off the wall.

Then I picked up one of the dustbins and raised it above my shoulders. The lid fell off clattering behind me.

I aimed the bin towards the glass. It hit the frame and crashed to the ground, spilling newspapers, cereal packets, tea leaves, potato peelings, old carrots. You name it.

My breathing was heavy. I could feel my heart thumping.

"HELLO!" I shouted. "IT'S SO NICE TO BE FUCKIN' HOME!"

As the rubbish bin rolled back towards me I gave it one almighty kick. The door remained shut.

Still huffing and puffing I stopped by the balcony in the hallway and tried to work out what to do next.

A small crowd had gathered on the landing as well as those same white kids from earlier who were sneering in my direction.

"And you lot can fuck off, too!" I screamed.

I stuck my head down and headed towards them. Everyone except for three white kids with the wraparound shades scattered. They held their ground.

"Go on, scram!" I said without easing up my pace.

The tallest one was leaning against a wall defiantly

so I jabbed a finger at him.

"I said, clear off."

The kid must have been about 17 or 18, wearing an orange shellsuit and a baseball cap. He grinned at me without an ounce of fear on his face. One gold tooth protruded from his crooked mouth.

"Yo' Karen's ol' man right?"

He spoke like a black man and that really got up my nose. Black guys talk like black guys and that's all well and good. So was this little prick taking the piss or what?

I grabbed two handfuls of his shellsuit and the chunky gold chain round his neck. Then I pulled him towards me.

"That's none of your fuckin' business."

"She my friend, man. She tol' be all 'bout ya' ..."

We stared into each other's eyes in a feeble face-off for a few moments.

"Yo' was called 'The boss', right?"

I ignored him.

"Chill out, Meester Boss."

Here I was, fresh out of nick and on a short leash. I took one long deep breath and let the air out through my nose.

Then I said quietly, "Go away."

The kid wasn't impressed. He moved quickly, quicker than I'd have given him credit for, twisted away from my grip and hooked an ankle behind my leg. Then he rabbit punched me with both fists. I stumbled backwards, cursing myself for letting myself get caught off guard. I recovered my balance and squared up to him.

He was no pushover. Before I reached him again he had his fists cocked, martial arts style, at his sides.

He landed a jackhammer right to my shoulder, but I managed to use the force of the blow to transfer all my weight onto my right leg.

I channelled every ounce of strength into a karate kick that hit the sweetest spot of all, just above his bread basket. He doubled over and I grabbed him by the belt and rammed him headfirst into the wall opposite the balcony.

He went down on both knees. I yanked his head back and was about to slam it against the wall even harder when his two mates jumped in. One of them wrapped his arms around both my legs, pulling me off the wall and sending me crashing onto my back.

Then one straddled my chest and started smashing his fist into my face. The other kid stamped his heel into the side of my head. Neither of them had the muscle to do any real damage to me but I wasn't hanging aroudn to wait and see if they got lucky. I wriggled free and was half sitting up when the first kid headed back into the action again, getting his forearm round my neck and pulling hard.

The one straddling me smacked a full swing into my stomach, but he'd come within range and I aimed a fresh fist right into his jaw. He fell to the side as I impacted.

Then I smacked my elbow into the bridge of the bigger kid's nose. My knee cut into the other kid's chin knocking him completely off balance. They were in a right fucking panic and all three of them knew they were in for a real hiding now. Then a familiar voice came from behind us.

"Hey, cool it ... cool it!"

The nearest kid took a swipe at me and missed just as a big black arm reached in and fended him off. My old mate Carl had come to the rescue.

"Show the man respect. Come on. Respect ..."

The soft West Indian accent, the mohair suit, the smell of after shave. I felt calm spreading all over me.

"... he could kill ya if he wanted. Ya dig?"

The white rastaboys stopped and looked up at Carl, all six foot five of him.

"Give de man some space. He just got outta nick."

As I got to my feet, the biggest of the three little shits jostled past me, brushing my shoulder. I crunched my fist into his stomach for good measure. He doubled up in pain and fell to the floor. I stood over him.

"Ya dig?" I muttered through gritted teeth as I looked down at him writhing about in agony, clutching his gut.

Then I aimed my right boot towards his kidneys. He rolled up in a ball as my leg swung towards him. I stopped in mid air, grinned and walked off.

Carl's great arm went around my shoulders as we moved towards the stairwell.

"Good ta see ya, Tony. Been a long time."

We walked down the stairs and out onto the street below Tavistock House.

"So, what's their game?" I asked Carl. I

straightened out my suit and poked at the minor scratches and grazes I'd picked up during the tussle.

"Dey run dis estate, man."

"Run it?"

"Tings 'ave changed since yo' went 'way, my friend."

I shook by head in bewilderment.

Carl continued: "Places like this are a no-go area. Police never come 'ere."

"I'm worried about my kid."

"Ya right ta worry."

Carl glanced back. The crowd had broken up. The youths had gone. The estate looked dead.

"Changes. Dat's de word, my friend. Lots o' changes."

"Does that mean you've changed?" I asked Carl.

He laughed. But then a smile was never far from my old mate's Carl's face.

3

"Yo' look real fit, man," said Carl as we walked through the estate's abandoned playground.

Then he clapped me on the back.

"Is so good ta see ya."

"D'you get that last book I sent you?"

"Yeah," Carl said. "But it shoulda been de wife who done it."

"Why?"

"'Cause women do every dam ting in dis world."

I laughed and clapped him on the back.

"Fair point, Carl. Fair point."

We'd walked half a mile from the estate. Carl no longer had his hand around my shoulder, but we were picking up where we last left off, enjoying that old familiar feeling you get with real mates. That's a feeling that is steady as Nelson's Column. With a real mate you can do the gossip, have a laugh or set the future to rights. If there is any future.

"The Hammers are doin' all right," I said to Carl.

When we were kids just about everyone on the manor supported West Ham — even Carl. Now that took some bottle for a black kid in the East End of the sixties. The colour predjudice on the terraces in those days was well out of order.

When the Hammers signed Clyde Best — one of the first black men to play in the old first division — those National Front bastards at the North End of Upton Park gave Carl and any other coloured people a terrible amount of stick. But he loyally stuck with the Hammers. And I loyally stuck with him.

One time when we was knocking round together in our teens, Carl asked me outright why I was mates with him when all the other white kids in the street avoided him like the plague.

I told him it wasn't hard — most of those kids hated me, too. I had a reputation as a bit of a psycho — a lot different from most of them. I didn't take any shit from them and they knew what they'd get if they started on me or any of mine. They gave me a wide berth but they'd shout or call me names when they thought they was at a safe distance, out of my reach. I knew what it was like to have people pointing the finger at me, giving me a hard time. But the grief that some of the kids gave me was nothing compared with what Carl got.

I soon realised while chatting to Carl that I should have looked him up first when I got out of the slammer. Then I could have eased myself back on the manor nice and slow. My problem is I've always steamed into things without a moment's thought — even after twelve years with time to plan every move.

Karen and Brenda had been eating a hole in my brain since the day she split from me. To be honest about it, I never thought she'd take me at my word and cut off all communications between us. All that business at the flat left me gutted.

We jumped in Carl's motor — a gleaming black BMW 5 series — and began driving up Vallance Road. I wondered what Carl had in store for me. He always surprised me, and I had twelve years of changes to catch up with.

Carl could be a right old ducker and diver, but he'd held on to his minicab business in a rundown old garage crammed under a railway arch just off the Dalston Road.

He kept a small flat across the street. But Carl also had a number of other homes for a number of ladies and his big brood of nippers. I never talked much about that with him because it wasn't none of my business.

It was the same with prison visits. Carl never came to see me because he was worried about one or two outstanding matters involving Plod.

But we swapped the occasional book because Carl and I were both big readers. In fact, he was the one who encouraged me to bury myself in books when I got sent down. That one piece of advice probably helped save my sanity.

A few minutes later we pulled up by his minicab office opposite the flat and I saw something I never thought I'd ever see again — my old silver Mercedes.

"Christ!" I said, not really believing what was in front of my eyes.

"What?" Carl said.

"You still got it!"

"'Course I have."

"Yeah, but I thought ..."

I'd told Carl years back to flog it and give the money to Brenda and Karen. He must have bunged them the cash out of his own pocket. What a fucking gent.

The old silver Merc was parked on a yellow line, standing under a tree. I jumped out of Carl's Beemer and headed over to it. I kept blinking my eyes and expecting it to disappear.

The old beauty had even been washed and polished, and the sun glinted off the silver paint and gleaming chrome trim.

I pressed the handle on the driver's side just as Carl strolled up alongside me.

"You keep it tuned?"

"What sorta question is dat? Is got MOT, new tyres, da works."

"Christ ..." I said, running my hand lightly over the paintwork. "I never thought I'd see her again."

Carl held out the key ring and I took it from him

and climbed inside the motor. It smelled of old leather, just like it always had.

I reached over to touch each of the knobs on the dashboard, felt the automatic gear lever, then adjusted the rear-view mirror, first to look at myself and then to angle it just right for driving.

Carl slid in beside me. The engine fired up first time. A magical, purring noise came from the V-8 under the bonnet and I slipped my sparkling Mercedes 280SE into D for Drive. As I pulled away from the kerb, I glanced at the mileometer.

"You been clockin' this, Carl?"

"Wot?"

"Ain't done many miles, according to this clock."

"Wot sorta question is dat? I been keepin' it fa ya. I got me own set o' wheels."

"Magic. Bloody magic."

I drove carefully and slowly for the first half-mile or so, then felt all my old instincts return. I took a little tour round all my old haunts. At last, I felt I was home.

Suddenly, Carl said out of the blue: "If I'd written it, de wife would 'ave been da one who did it."

"What?"

"Da book, man."

"Oh ... the book," I said, "but if she'd done it then it would have been too obvious."

"But she could 'ave cut da body up and fed it ta de sharks."

"Too fuckin' obvious."

Carl laughed.

"It's all in the plot, my friend," I said, knowingly.

"You gotta do the opposite of what everyone expects, otherwise they'll see it comin'."

With my free hand I leaned across, opened the glove compartment and rattled around looking for something.

"How 'bout some sounds?"

Carl shrugged, but without taking notice of his reply I slipped a dusty old cassette into the machine. The tape came on in the middle of The Temptations' "Papa Was A Rolling Stone."

I took a deep, satisfied breath, straightened my arms and pressed my shoulders back against the soft leather seat. Carl nodded to the soul beat. He'd turned me onto to it all when we'd been kids.

But as the music wafted through the air, it got me thinking about Brenda again.

"Why does she hate me so much, Carl?"

"She don't hate yo', man."

"'Course she does."

"Is a woman ting. Yo never can tell with women. Dey different. Dey wear high heels. Dey like ta powder dere noses and dey go ta Heaven."

"Unlike us."

"You got it!" he said slapping the dash in front of him.

I laughed and clapped him on the thigh.

Just then I noticed one of the shops we were driving past. I braked and pulled over to the side. Carl looked across at me, wondering what the hell I was doing.

"Hold the fort," I said to Carl.

I swung the door open and almost had it smashed

off by a passing bus. Then I ducked across the road and headed into a sports shop about thirty yards behind us.

The sweet smell of linseed oil used to remind me of the fight game when I visited the same shop in the old days.

But now there wasn't a boxing glove in sight — just row after row of footballs, football boots and club kits. Eventually I spotted a punchbag and some gloves in the far corner of the shop.

Twelve years back it had been the other way around. It certainly summed up the sorry state of the fight game by the time I was allowed back into the so-called real world.

"Got any white pigskin gloves?" I asked the little Indian fellow behind the counter.

"Sorry, sir?" he replied

"White pigskin boxing gloves. You got any?"

"Oh, yes sir. I look for you."

He moved to the other end of the counter and climbed up a ladder before grabbing hold of a largish cardboard box. He climbed back down, brushed the dust off the lid and pulled it open.

"They gotta be white," I said, before he'd even pulled them out.

"Abolutely, sir," he replied nervously.

I peered inside the box.

"They'll do."

The gloves cost me £85, which was most of what I had left in my pocket.

Back in the Merc I passed them to Carl, who

laughed when he pulled them out of the box.

"Tony, how dese gonna help ya?"

He took them out, shaking his head as he spoke.

"I told ya, man. Tings have changed while yo been 'way."

"Not that much, they haven't."

I started the car up again and pulled out into the traffic, driving faster than before. I was thinking about everything and now I knew exactly where I wanted to go.

4

I stopped the Merc at the opening of a short dead end lane just off the Durnsford Road, east of Hoxton town centre. I wound down the window, and stared at a neon sign flickering at the far end of the street. In the gloomy grey daylight it all looked pretty bloody depressing.

The Kentucky Club, on and off, on and off. The Kentucky Club. It looked like a real dive.

"Don't go in, man," Carl said as I slung the silver merc up on the curb.

"It's gotta be done."

"I told ya, tings are different."

"And Benny?" I asked. "Is he different, too?"

"Completely, my friend. Completely." He was shaking his head again. "De rules 'ave changed, Tony."

"Mine haven't."

I reached over and plucked the white gloves from Carl's lap.

"Ya tink Benny cares?"

"He's got to, ain't he?" I said as I got out of the car.

Then I headed off down the street.

The door to the club was closed, but not locked. I let myself in, and followed the steps down to a basement. It whiffed of last night's booze and stale piss.

Inside it was dusty and dark. Just what I expected. If the lights had been turned up I'd probably have seen the dampness dripping off the walls. The place was kitted out with crummy plastic furniture and Indian restaurant wallpaper.

I moved across the room holding the gloves under my arm but keeping them out of sight. In the poor light I bumped into a table, grating it across the wooden floor. At that moment the only other person in the room turned in my direction.

It was a girl, slouched on a bar stool, twirling a straw sticking out of a drink in a tall glass. She had long blonde hair and was wearing a skimpy white top. It was cut short so you could see the stud pierced through her belly button. Why do people do that to themselves? She also had a skinny-looking blue tiger tattooed on her upper arm — okay for sailors, truck drivers and arse bandits, fucking terrible on a young girl.

She looked up, glanced at me, then turned back to her drink almost immediately.

"We're closed ..." she slurred her words. "Open at

six. Come back then."

"I'm lookin' for someone ..." I said.

"Del, tell 'im," she interrupted.

Just then out of the shadows came a tall, heavy-set bloke. He was wearing black trousers and a pristine white cotton shirt. Looked like it was part of a DJ he probably wore night-times.

"We're closed," he paused, "Sir."

"Hello, Del," I said. "How's it going?"

I stepped under a dusty overhanging spotlight, holding the white gloves in my hands. It was only then he could see me more clearly.

"Bloody hell," Del said. "You been away a while."

"Mine's a half a lager ... none of that bottled rubbish ... please."

I gently placed the gloves on the bar.

"When did you get out?" asked Del.

"This morning."

"You don't hang about do you?"

"Thought I'd look up some old mates," I replied, but I didn't like the tone of his voice.

"Things 'ave changed round 'ere."

"Not everythin', Del," I said. "Not everythin'."

"What?" he said, squinting at me in a way that always gets me going.

"You heard me," I snapped back.

"You're not the fuckin' Boss no more," replied Del.

"You reckon?" I said.

Then I whacked him half strength right in the kisser. He wobbled and then fell to the floor. I stood over him with a boot on his chest.

"I'm lookin' for Benny, Del. When I want your opinions I'll ask for them ..."

I glanced around at the rundown bar.

"... it's funny thinkin' this place used to be a half decent gym with some half decent geezers." I paused. "Looks and smells more like a fuckin' chippie now."

I paused and stared down at Del, who was still struggling under my right boot.

"So where the fuck is he?"

"What?" he muttered breathlessly.

I took a long deep intake of air through my nostrils.

"I got some news for you, Del ..." I said, pressing my boot harder into his chest.

I shifted all my weight onto my right leg and felt it sink deeper into his chest. Nothing too heavy, just showing him who was in charge.

"The Boss is back and he's lookin' for Benny," I said.

Del was struggling for breath now.

"He's not around."

"So where is he?"

"You'd better ask Henry."

He nodded towards a half-drawn curtain at the darker end of the bar. I could see a door beyond it.

I picked up my gloves and moved quickly across the bar. My eyes had now got used to the gloomy light, and I walked around the scattered tables and chairs with special care this time.

I felt better now. I was starting to come alive again. All the old instincts were kicking in. I was still somebody who deserved a bit of respect.

Del had been right in one way: things had changed.

The fight game had died and all the blokes involved in it had moved into much dodgier territory. But one thing remained the same; fear ruled.

I pushed aside the curtain and went through. There was a small office with daylight glinting from above. Pictures of naked birds were hanging from the walls: not crumpet pictures, like in a calender, but as if they were on display, part of the staff. A geezer was leaning over a desk, jabbing away at a computer keyboard.

He looked up as I entered.

I said: "Hallo, Henry."

His thoughts were still obviously more on the computer than me. He squinted back into the glowing screen. I immediately noticed he looked different. Not only older but more smartly dressed. I'd never seen him in a suit before.

"You musta heard I was out, then?" I asked.

The computer started beeping before he could answer. The screen cleared, then a long list of numbers scrolled down from the bottom and vanished into oblivion. Henry reached over and hit a key, and the whole display froze instantly.

"Fuckin' thing does my brain in."

He then turned and grimaced at me.

"Once upon a time we were all just honest villains," he said. "Now I've gotta deal with all this computer bollocks."

"So where is he?"

"Benny's away. Costa Del Sol."

"Oh yeah?"

"We've all moved on, Tony. It's not like the old days."

"I'm fuckin' bored of people tellin' me that, Henry," I paused. "Benny owes me. Said he'd look after me. I took a fuckin' long fall for him."

I held up the pristine white kid leather boxing gloves and lay them on the table.

"Well," I said, "when you see him, give him these. He'll know what I want."

I thrust the gloves across at Henry who was so surprised he accepted them without question.

"The way I'd hoped it would go back in those days ..." I said, "... was that I'd fight until me chin turned to glass and then join the backroom staff."

I didn't bother waiting for an answer. I pushed my way back through the curtain and walked into the main part of the club.

Del was standing at the bar talking to the girl. I gave him the evil eye and he immediately looked away. I felt like whacking him again but there wasn't much point.

I'd just reached the bottom of the steps when I heard Henry calling after me.

"Tony!"

I turned back.

"What?"

"Let's have a word."

"Not if you're gonna waste my fuckin' time again."

Henry shook his head. As we walked back into his office the computer was buzzing again. He leaned down and hit another key. This time the screen flickered and then went blank.

"Fuck it," he said.

"What you tryin' to do?"

"Get back to the main menu."

"Out the way," I said.

I reached past him and tapped on the keys at the same time. The disk drive fired up again.

Then it turned itself off and the screen cleared leaving the main menu display. The cursor blinked up at us.

"How d'you manage that, then?" Henry asked.

"You learn all sorts of useful things in the nick. You should try it some time."

Henry reached in his pocket. "Got somethin' for you ..."

He chucked me a mobile phone. I caught it and weighed it up in my hand.

"Good communications, Tony. That's the key to everythin' these days."

"You reckon?" I said.

"Keep it on you at all times," he said, ignoring my remark. "We'll be in touch."

Henry's comment reminded me how I'd paid the ultimate price for Benny's "bad communications" back in the old days.

5

18 May 1987 is the day that shaped this entire story.

A lot of people don't believe in a sixth sense but I've got no doubt you know when things are about to happen — good and bad.

I'd just left my lovely five-bedroomed detached house in Chigwell to head over to the Tiger Gym, in Hoxton. It was the boiler-room of my career in the fight game.

The day began like any other. Our little daughter Karen had woken me up with the birds and Brenda was worn out after having to deal with her during the night. I fed Karen breakfast to give Brenda a break but by the time she'd chucked half her porridge on the floor I couldn't wait to get out of the house and away from all that domestic stuff.

When I finally got in my motor I was already well wound up from the strain of fatherhood. Seems stupid of me looking back on it now. I didn't realise just how bloody lucky I was at the time.

I'd arranged to meet my trainer, Charlie Ferguson, for a big session to get me sharpened up for a bout I was due to fight a couple of days later against a gypo called Jimmy "The Tank" Fraser.

I was driving on the old A10 — which is always bumper-to-bumper into town — listening to the radio when I had this strange feeling come over me. Something wasn't right. But I couldn't put my finger on what it was.

Half an hour later I slung the motor up in the car park behind the gym. It was right next to a funeral parlour, just off the Shallots Road in the heart of my old manor.

As I was strolling in, I noticed a couple of dodgy-looking blokes parked nearby in a black Granada. They looked like the law, which wasn't unusual as there was quite a few faces using the gym in those days. My promoter Benny Davis — who also owned the Tiger Gym as well as just about every half-decent scrapper in East London — had a bit of form as well.

When I walked in that morning Charlie was already setting up my favourite brown soft leather punchbag. I had a heavy session, sweated buckets and bruised my knuckles.

But I was buzzing with fitness when, three hours

later, I got back in my motor and headed home. Then I noticed those same geezers in the black Granada in my rear view.

As I turned into a side-road that I often used as a short cut about a mile or so from the gym, the Granada came right up my arse, if you know what I mean.

Seconds later the bastards were trying to ram me. I wasn't having any of that. I slammed on my brakes and they just managed to avoid going in my back.

I carried on driving and they did it again. This time I swerved right across them and pulled up in the middle of the street.

I jumped out.

"What the fuck's your game?" I screamed at these two geezers as they got out of the Granada.

One of them had a shooter in his hand. Maybe they weren't the law after all?

"Get in the motor," said the one waving the gun.

"What?" I said.

"Get in the fuckin' car. NOW!"

"Fuck off," I snapped back, still sweating from my workout.

He aimed the gun right at me.

"You gonna do me in broad daylight?" I said to them defiantely.

The one with the gun moved closer to me.

"Just fuckin' get in."

I still stood my ground. The moment I looked in this bloke's eyes I knew he didn't have the bottle to pull the trigger.

He moved closer to try and intimidate me. But all that did was put him within my striking distance. I glanced across at his mate, who was much smaller and looked even more twitchy.

I nailed him across the bridge of his nose with all my strength. Then I kicked out at his hand and the shooter went flying. I made a grab for it.

Just as I reached it the other bastard jumped me. We got in a bear hug but I twisted him round and tried to throw him out of the way. The piece went off. He crumpled to the ground.

His mate scrambled backwards away from me. He was shit scared of the thing in my right hand. He dived behind a hedge and I turned and walked back towards my car.

It wasn't until I got near my car I realised I still had the shooter in my hand. I looked around and there was no one in sight.

I glanced behind me and over my shoulder. I fumbled in my pocket to find my car keys. Finally I lurched into the motor, shaking like a bloody leaf. Those two dickheads had really wound me up. I hate dealing with shooters. I didn't know whether the prat I'd accidentally nailed with the shooter was dead or alive although he acted pretty fucking dead to me when he keeled over. I certainly wasn't fucking well waiting around to find out. I threw the piece on the seat beside me and turned the ignition key.

At that moment Old Bill appeared at the end of the road. Call it bad luck or good planning. I don't know which to this day.

There was a stiff lying by the side of the road and I was trying to scarper. It didn't look good. I could try and make a run for it or simply roll over. That was when I made the biggest mistake of my life.

Within seconds, I was face down eating dirt with a knee in my back being read my rights.

"Anthony Francis Mills (they even knew my bloody middle name), I am arresting you on suspicion of murder. You are not obliged to say anything but what you do say will be taken down and used in evidence against you."

The next day I was up in court being remanded in custody. It turned out the two geezers who'd rammed my car were plain-clothes Old Bill.

My promoter, Benny Davies, immediately coughed up for a brief. Then I got word it was him and some of his boys they were after for some armed robbery over in Barking.

Turned out Benny had handled the loot after financing the entire operation. Some grass had put the finger on me as being suspect numero uno.

I had a choice — take the fall or take a swim off Blackfriars Bridge, and nobody swims too well with their feet chained to a concrete block. The unwritten agreement was that I'd be looked after when I got out and all my legal bills would be taken care of.

My trial at the Old Bailey only lasted three days. My brief said I would have to plead guilty to manslaughter otherwise they'd get me for murder.

The only witness was the other detective —

whose best mate I'd killed. I knew I'd be going away, but everyone reckoned it would be a maximum five-stretch for what was an accidental death, after all.

But the Judge who presided over my sentencing was a snotty-looking bastard who peered at me over his poncy little wire-rimmed glasses as he summed up. "You challenged two policemen and, as a result, one of them died. I have to deter other people from ever doing this. Anthony Francis Mills, you are a menace to society and you will go to prison for 12 years."

I couldn't believe what I was hearing. But the Judge hadn't finished yet.

"I recommend you serve the entire sentence as a lesson to others."

Twelve fucking years for killing someone by accident. He might as well have given me a life sentence.

Naturally, the newspapers all had a field day. They dubbed me an "East End thug who'd got what he deserved".

I made the front page of every rag the day after my trial ended. Only good thing about it was that when I got in the slammer my so-called reputation preceded me. The judge said I was a menace to society. A man not to be crossed.

The irony of all this is I couldn't have grassed up Benny even if I'd wanted to on account of the fact I didn't know sweet FA about the blagging his team had carried out.

Mind you, it's often crossed my mind that the man himself set me up as some kind of sacrificial lamb, if you know what I mean.

6

So here I was twelve years later being told by everyone that the world had changed, but it hadn't. Not really. On the surface it might have, but the slags and scumbags were still the same. Benny still owed me. Henry was still a slippery bastard. Del ran a clip joint instead of a boxing gym ... and Carl still helped out his mates, whatever their colour.

"You're one hell of a survivor, ain't you," I said to Carl, as we sat in the front room of his flat.

"Keep a low profile. Dat's my way, man."

"Wish I knew how to," I said.

Carl ignored that and flicked on a remote control. The wide screen telly came to life.

I looked around and remembered how it had been in Carl's place before computers and wide screen TVs.

Some of the furniture was still the same as years ago. That made it feel a bit like home, or as near as I could get to it under the circumstances.

The key to Carl's survival had always been that he had a lot of order in his life. He was the original man-with-a-plan.

He'd planned his own fight career out carefully until we met in the ring a couple of years before I got banged up. He lost but — as we'd been mates since we were kids — I wasn't proud of beating him. I told him to walk away from the fight game and get a decent job.

Carl went into the import/export lark and took to it like the proverbial duck to water. On the personal front, as I've mentioned, Carl had two or three ladies scattered about the place, including one on the estate where Brenda and Karen lived.

Me and Carl had been out and around the East End most of the day and I was knackered. It had been a long day for someone more used to twenty hours a day in a cell. I was just about to sink into one of his armchairs and split open a can of beer when he said:

"Got somet'ing ta show ya."

"What's that then?" I said wearily.

"Follow me."

He led me out of the flat across the street to a lock-up alongside the minicab office. He flicked on a naked light bulb hanging from the ceiling. There in the corner were about 500 boxes, clearly marked with the words BURGLAR ALARMS.

"Wot yo' reckon?" Carl said.

"I think you got a load of nicked burglar alarms."

"Dey gonna sell like hot cakes, man."

Carl picked up one of the boxes, and handed it to me. I opened it carefully.

"I paid £2 each. Can ya believe dat? Dey worth at least £50," said Carl.

"Where's the instructions?" I said, digging around the box.

"Dey ain't got none."

"No instructions?"

"Is no' problem."

"How's anyone goin' to make 'em work?"

Carl just winked. "I tell ya. Is no problem."

I side-stepped any involvement in Carl's dodgy produce. He could tell from the look on my face I had other problems on my plate.

A few minutes later Carl was conjuring up some grub in the kitchen while I sat in the lounge thinking about Brenda and Karen. Then my mind turned to Benny.

Those three people held the key to my future, whether I liked it or not. I took the mobile phone out of my pocket and examined it.

"They used to smuggle these things into the nick," I called over to Carl. "But I never had no-one worth phoning."

His head poked out from the kitchen. He had a smudge of yellow curry paste on the corner of his mouth.

"Yo' can't live widout dem dese days."

"That's what they said about shooters in the old

days."

Carl ignored that last remark because he knew the real reason why I was handling the phone.

"They'll call yo' when dey want yo'."

Carl took the mobile out of my hand and looked at it. There was a number on the back which had been stuck on with Sellotape.

"Ya need ta learn dis else some dude gonna steal it and use it fa demselves."

Then he handed it back.

"What d'you press when it rings."

But Carl had already disappeared back into the kitchen.

Just then the mobile started singing. I nearly dropped it out of my hand with shock.

"Bloody hell!"

Carl reappeared with his own phone glued to his ear.

"It works."

He flicked off his own phone and my one stopped singing.

"Ya can turn de volume down," said Carl. "Here, give it ta me." He took it from me and started fiddling around.

"Ya want de National Anthem or de Beatles?"

"You what?" I said.

"Ringin' tone. What d'ya like?"

I shrugged my shoulders. I didn't give a toss. Lot more important things to worry about.

"Make sure ya keep de batteries charged up every day ..." Carl then paused, "... and don't mess wid

Benny."

"I told you, I got things to get sorted."

"They ain't ever goin' to get sorted."

"But he owes me."

"So wot?"

"They said he was in Spain," I called after Carl. "He might not even know I'm out yet."

Carl didn't respond.

A few moments later he yelled. "I nearly forgot. Dere's sometin' for yo' on the sideboard."

"What?"

"On the sideboard. A book."

I picked it up: it was a paperback of a novel by American crime writer James Ellroy.

"Thanks, Carl. Any good?"

Carl appeared, carrying two plates of steaming hot curry.

"He make yo' realise yo' ain't so badly off."

Then he gave one of the plates of curry to me.

"Curry's good for ya. Get ya good and strong."

"I'm already good and strong."

"I'm talkin' 'bout ya head, my friend."

Carl sat down, and started shovelling food into his mouth.

"De book's 'bout some dude's who's killin' golf caddies. After each murder de cops find a golf ball stuffed in dere mouths."

"Sounds a bit fuckin' gruesome to me," I said.

"Bit like ya', Tony. Ain't it?"

I sidestepped his last comment. I pinned the book open against the table with my elbow and began reading while I ate.

Next day, around four in the afternoon, I drove my silver Merc down a side street in Hoxton. There was nowhere to park, so I stopped in the middle of the road, letting the engine tick over.

On my right was a vast five-tier council estate. Graffiti was daubed across most of the ground floor walls. I still didn't have a fucking clue what any of the fancy writing meant. Maybe I would have to get Carl to give me a crash course once I had taken care of business.

A long brick wall sectioned the estate off from some modern, private housing on the other side. For a moment it reminded me of the nick and I started to think that I was just having a dream, that I would wake up back inside. Your mind can play bloody strange tricks on you. Good job it's on your side most of the time.

Just after four, a bunch of schoolkids started pouring out from a big gate between two walls ... both sexes, all sizes, colours and shapes. My eyes perked up, and I scanned the young faces as they milled past the car.

Then I saw her, walking silently along with a group of her mates, her eyes pointing at the pavement. She looked tired. Maybe Brenda had given her a hard time after what happened the day before.

As Karen passed the car, I looked towards her, hoping to catch her eye. But she didn't even look up, and I didn't have the courage to call out her name because I was afraid she might be angry.

Within a few seconds Karen had disappeared out of sight amongst a crowd of other schoolkids.

I sat there in stony silence and felt the tears welling up in my eyes. Soppy, eh? Grisly old bastard like me on the verge of blubbing like a baby. I don't need to justify how I felt to anyone but that girl was my motivation. The thought of maybe being able to be a father to her again had kept me going through twelve long years. She was my blood. And then there was her mother ...

Just then this loud beeping noise went off, and I nearly jumped out of my skin.

I swore out loud and yanked it out of my inside jacket pocket. I found the green button Carl had shown me and pressed it.

A man's voice said: "We got work for you," and then hung up.

7

The voice at the other end of the mobile gave me an address in Clerkenwell. I scratched through my ancient, yellowing A-Z and soon found the place — a converted warehouse block in a narrow street. It looked a lot different from the last time I was in this part of the manor.

I pressed the door buzzer and there was a long silence. After the third press I finally got a response.

The woman who answered only said, "Third floor" and then there was a different buzzing noise and the door opened. I went in, the door shut behind me and a second door buzzed open in front. The place was like a fucking high security unit. They even had closed circuit TV cameras pointed at me. I had to remind myself that this wasn't to lock people in, it was to keep undesirables out. Mind you, who were they expecting? The S-A-fucking-S?

The hallway was bare with white walls and wooden floors. It felt cold and empty. The woman was standing by the front door of her flat with her arms folded. She nodded her head towards almost a dozen cardboard cartons covered in South African apple stamps.

I lifted one of them and immediately realised they were full of bottles of booze. The woman then moved closer and stood, hands on hips, watching me.

"Careful you don't break anything."

"Have I got to carry this bleedin' lot all on my own?" I said.

"You'll manage," was all she replied.

I humped the first box out of the flat, down the stairs, through those pain-in-the-arse doors and out to my old motor.

Then I realised I'd left the boot locked and had to drop the carton on the pavement. I sucked a mouthful of air through my teeth, did the honours and then heaved the box into the boot. I did a total of nine return trips up and down those stairs.

On the final run the woman followed me down and then stood on the steps watching me as I heaved the last box into the back of the Merc.

"Where's this lot gotta go then?" I asked.

"Address is on that last box ..." She turned to go back into the flats. "... you can read, can't you?"

The door slammed behind her. I muttered something in her direction but luckily she never heard it. If she'd been a bloke I'd have planted one on her. I yanked open the back door and pushed the box around until I found the address scrawled on the side.

The drop-off point turned out to be a crummy little lock-up behind King's Cross Station, the sort of place where people get up to no good. A Latino looking spiv was waiting at the entrance when I rolled up. He just wagged a finger in the direction of where he wanted me to put the boxes in a corner of the pitch dark garage.

When I'd dumped the lot, I asked him, "What now?"

"What?"

I didn't like the cold look on his face one little bit.

"Haven't you gotta sign for it, or somethin'?"

"Nah," he said, glaring at me. So I pulled out of there.

I knew from my mates in the slammer that booze and fags had become a major "business" while I'd been away. In the old days, bootlegging was nothing more than a hobby to most people but the illegal importation of tax-free fags and booze had turned into a multi-million pound industry during the nineties, thanks to their escalating price here at home.

The operation was simple; by bringing lorryloads of fags and booze directly from France to Kent and London and then selling them on, you could avoid paying any British taxes. It had become quite a tidy earner for a lot of East End firms.

And I was being used to ferry the smaller, special deliveries once they got into the smoke and needed careful distribution.

Just then the mobile started singing again and a voice told me about my second job of the day.

Later that same evening, I left my Merc in the garage of a posh hotel near Canary Wharf, in the Docklands, and took a spin through the revolving door of the main entrance.

A commissionaire was standing there looking a right pillock in his spotless green uniform with a shiny top hat balanced on his head. He had a pair of immaculate white gloves clutched in his right hand. I'd noticed this before: doormen outside fancy hotels always hold their gloves, never wear them. One day I'd get round to asking one why.

As I passed him, this particular pillock muttered: "Good evening, sir."

"Good evening," I replied, wondering if he was after a tip.

The doorman looked down at my shoes so I looked down at his. They were black and shiny while mine were, I have to admit, a bit scuffed, on account of them being more than 12 years old.

Once in the main lobby I noticed the reception desk was staffed by three well turned out women. There was an arcade with a jewellery store, a news stand and a shop filled with fancy leather goods. There were also glass cases positioned against various walls containing expensive looking china and watches and stuff. I'd never seen anything quite like it and was having a good old butchers when I realised that people were looking at me gawping. Oh, dear. Maybe they'd think that this scruffy looking item in the ancient suit, beaten-up shoes and boxer's face was 'casing the joint' or some other such phrase that they'd heard in some TV gangster movie. I calmed myself down and tried to look invisible.

The lobby was the main meeting point of the hotel and there were lots of small tables arranged in carefully screened-off corners, surrounded by potted plants. The thickly carpeted hall led through fancy arches to all of the different areas of the hotel.

There were signs for two restaurants, a tea room, the lifts, and so on. In the middle of the lobby was a grand double staircase. The bannisters were painted gold and the stair rods were gleaming as nicely as my freshly polished Merc. Hanging from the ceiling above the stairwell was a big crystal chandelier.

Just then I heard the sound of a three-piece band playing tunes that even I remembered from before I was banged up. I spotted a white-coated waiter and walked up to him.

"Where's the bar?" I asked.

The waiter, a prissy looking nonce in his early twenties, looked ever so politely at me.

"If you'd care to take a seat,sir, I'd be pleased to serve you."

"Half a lager, please."

"Take a seat please, sir."

I frowned at him, then backed away. I spotted an empty table and chair and moved towards it. I stood out like a fucking nun in a stripclub. So much for looking invisible. I tried to sit down carefully and even crossed my legs before looking over at the waiter again.

Then he minced over again with a notepad in his hand and a silver tray under his arm.

"Something to drink, sir?"

"Told you ... half a lager, please."

"We only do bottled beers, sir."

"What?"

"Only bottled, sir."

"That'll do."

The waiter scribbled something out on his pad, resting it on his silver tray, then walked away gingerly. I noticed his hair was drawn back into a ponytail, tied with an elastic band. Waiters couldn't get away with that in the days before I was sent down.

The drink turned up sooner than I expected and was placed in front of me with a paper serviette and a bright green piece of lime that I immediately dumped in the ashtray. I knocked it back quickly and then started looking around, wondering who I was going to meet.

I spotted a man in a dark suit. He walked slowly past my table a couple of times, looking at me a bit strangely. Second time round I grinned at him and raised my glass. That got rid of the fucker.

Then four Arabs swept through the lobby, trailed by a number of women in black veils. Moments later I smelt their sweet perfumes wafting past me.

"Another drink, sir?"

The same waiter was back within seconds of my last sip of lager.

"Yeah, please."

"And this time?"

"What about this time?"

"Your drink?" the waiter said, his ballpoint at the ready.

"Another bottle of lager," I said, "but don't bother with the green lemon. Think it's off."

"Yes, sir."

Yet again I got my order less than a minute later. Maybe they were trying to get rid of me?

"That's seven pounds fifty, sir."

"What makes you think I've finished?"

"Take your time, sir."

I fished in my pocket and pulled out a crumpled tenner. I handed it to the pony-tailed penguin, who made a right song and dance of searching slowly for the change. I stood my ground, and watched as my two pound fifty pence change was counted out in his hand and then placed on a tiny silver plate.

"Thanks," I said, sweeping all the change into the palm of my hand.

"Thank you, sir."

This time I sipped at my drink and absorbed all this richness around me. I could tell the staff thought I was a fish out of water and kept flashing me a lot of snotty glances.

I noticed the man in the dark suit from earlier looking me up and down again and realised he was probably the hotel detective.

I was only half way through my second bottle of lager when a pretty looking girl caught my eye.

She was on the upper landing, walking quickly towards the stairs. At first I thought she was starkers, but as she came into full view I saw she was wearing a tight strapless dress, covered in shiny blue stones. At the head of the stairs she stopped and put on a big leather coat that went right down to her ankles and seemed about three sizes too big for her.

Then she strode down those stairs like a girl on a mission. Long, thick dark curls flowed freely round her neat little face. She moved confidently down the steps despite her six inch heels.

But she wouldn't be interested in an old lag like me. I was more than forty years of age, complete with razor crop, thick neck and nasty manner. I knew my place in the world.

But I still carried on watching her because she was a very beautiful girl.

When she got to the lobby she glanced towards me and then moved even more quickly across the floor on those spikey heels.

When she was only a few feet away from me, the house detective in the dark suit stepped right up to her.

"On business, are we?" he said quietly, but very clearly.

The girl ignored him, and tried to brush past him. But he wasn't going to give up that easily.

"Can I help you, madam?"

He grabbed her elbow, but she wrenched it away angrily. Then she stepped past him and descended on me with a lovely smile forced across her pretty face.

"Sorry I took so long, darling."

She bent towards me and planted a wet juicy kiss full on my lips and then whispered: "Jimmy's on his way down but he wants us to wait in the car for him."

I could see the detective hovering behind her.

The girl took my arm and virtually pulled me to my feet. I didn't move at first. Then she whispered in my ear: "For fuck's sake move it!"

"What ...?"

"Hurry up, darling," she said out loud. "Otherwise we're going to be late."

Her fingernails dug into my arm as she steered me towards the main door, but her face still had that same glowing smile on it. People were staring at us by now.

It was like some kind of fucking pantomime as we tried to go through the revolving door — it hadn't been designed for two people at once. As we passed the commissionaire I nodded to him politely and even managed another glance at his posh shoes.

"Where's the car?" asked the girl.

"The Merc ... over there."

I tried to move away from her, but she caught my arm again.

"Pretend you know me," she said quietly, but I could tell she was getting angry.

"But I don't know you."

"Then pretend you fuckin' do!"

If there's one thing I don't like to hear it is women swearing but I didn't respond.

When we reached the car, I opened the back door for her. She reached past me and slammed it shut.

"Not the fuckin' back. I get in the front!"

"Suit yourself."

I walked round to the driver's side, climbed in, and then unlocked the passenger door from the inside. She slid in beside me.

"Where the hell did Benny get you from?" she spat at me.

Then she stared out of the window, with her back towards the hotel. The stuck-up commissionaire was looking right at us.

Just then my new part-time employer, Jimmy "The Mole" Melcham, came bounding towards us.

His nickname made total sense: short and stocky, small beady black eyes, a long nose with a red blob on the end and the sort of elderly, flabby skin I associate more with stiffs laid out in a morgue.

As he pulled open the car door he hissed at me. "Just get this fuckin' old heap on the road."

8

"Next time ... be on fuckin' time!" Jimmy The Mole screamed at me as we drove away from the hotel.

"Next time tell me what the hell's goin' on," I shouted back.

The Mole ignored me and then said breathlessly, "We got four more boozers to get to tonight."

"Bloody marvellous. But where are we going?"

"The Clarendon on Dalston High Street."

I let out a long sigh and swung the car right. Another vehicle was coming in the other direction. I swerved to avoid it. The girl was thrown against the door.

"Jesus!" she cried.

"Sorry."

"Keep your eyes on the fuckin' road," said The Mole angrily.

A couple of minutes of silence followed then The Mole started up again.

"Didn't you know you were supposed to be lookin' after me?"

"I was just told to meet a fellow at that hotel."

It transpired that one of Benny's people had put me up as a piece of muscle for some evening work for this chippy little midget Jimmy "The Mole" Melcham.

After making the briefest of introductions, he snorted at me: "Saw you knock out Taffy Holmes in Shoreditch a few years back."

"Yeah?" I said, relieved that at least I had something in common with the little twat.

"What were you known as back then?"

"The Boss."

"That's right. The Boss. Bet you wish you still was ..."

I knew he was winding me up but I didn't bite back. I just gave him one of my coldest jailhouse stares to let him know I'd sussed what his game was all about.

Just then his lady friend snapped on the interior light and grabbed at my rear-view so she could check herself over. She combed her hair, flicked gloss on her lips, then peered closely into the mirror to see if her eye make-up was okay.

"So what's your name, then?" I asked her.

"Mind your own fuckin' business," snapped Jimmy The Mole from the back.

I sucked a big mouthful of air in through my teeth and let out a big sigh. Somehow I was managing not to rise to the bait.

Best means of attack was to ignore them.

I went back to concentrating on my driving. His bird gave me my rear-view mirror back just before we dropped her off at a block of flats east of Dalston High Street. I never did catch her name.

Less than an hour later I was sitting, bored out my brains, in the bar of the Clarendon Arms, with a half of lager in front of me. Jimmy The Mole eventually reappeared from a meeting he'd had with the pub guv'nor. He even looked reasonably happy as he walked towards me.

"What's your poison?" I asked.

"No time for that. We got more people to see."

I knocked back my drink, stood up and moved alongside him and we walked off towards the exit.

Once we got back in the motor, I asked, "Where to now?"

"Loughton."

"Loughton, please?"

"Whatever ..." he said.

I pulled away. Just after we got on the Mile End Road I took my tape out of the glove compartment and slid it into the player.

The Temptations and "Papa Was A Rolling Stone" came wafting out of the speakers.

"Turn it off, will ya?"

"Don't you like it?"

"No I fuckin' don't."

"Well, that's your fuckin' problem," I sneered back.

"It's yours while you're workin' for me."

He reached over the back seat and hit the eject button on the cassette player.

I gripped the steering wheel tensely but didn't respond. For the following few minutes we drove in silence.

Then I thought, fuck it, there's no harm in asking, surely.

"So you're one of Benny's milkmen, then?"

He didn't respond at first but I could tell he didn't like me referring to 'the milk round' — collecting protection money.

"Just keep your eyes on the road," came the eventual reply.

"Just makin' conversation."

"Don't bother."

He took a cigarette from his pocket.

"Got a light?"

"You can't smoke in here."

"Why the fuck not?"

"'Cause I say so."

"I'll do what I fuckin' like."

"I'm still the boss in my own fuckin' motor and I don't wanna be poisoned by that shit."

"Poison you?" He paused. "Take more than a fuckin' cigarette to poison you."

I grabbed the neck of his shirt with one hand while the other stayed on the steering wheel.

"Don't fuckin' push it, mate."

I had him squashed up against the ceiling of the Merc as I carried on driving with the other hand.

"I been away a long time but that doesn't mean I don't deserve a bit of respect ..."

I still held up there.

"... I don't like people telling me what to do. D'you understand?"

He nodded slowly so I let him free.

I knew I was pushing my luck but there's only so much fucking lip I can take off anyone.

We sat there in silence for a few minutes. He probably thought I was going to pop him. But I let him off the hook.

Then I broke the wall of silence by pressing the automatic lighter on the walnut fascia. When it popped out I stabbed it in his direction. Felt like stubbing it out in his face.

He took it and lit up his fag as he rolled down the window. Then he glanced out of the window at the passing houses.

"Turn right here, then next left."

We'd driven into a much posher area. Sort of place where you'd need at least a million quid, just to drive down the road.

"Not a lot of boozers round here?"

"In here."

It was the gravel driveway to a large detached house set well back from the road. Jimmy The Mole directed me to park at the side of the house in an area where the gravel had been laid in a wide apron.

The moment I cut the engine, The Mole opened his

door and got out. He looked back at me and said, "Fifteen."

"Hours or minutes?"

He didn't reply and moved off towards the house.

I watched him closely. As he got near the door, it opened but I couldn't see clearly who was behind it. Then it closed.

I watched for a bit longer, hoping there'd be something more to see. At one point the shadows of two people were silhouetted against the curtained window. But nothing else. I slotted my one and only cassette tape back into the player, and settled back to wait.

I fell into a sort of daze then, which was only interrupted when The Mole began angrily tapping on my window. My eyes snapped open. I ejected the tape and leaned over to push open the door for him. He totally ignored me and sat in the back seat.

I noticed a figure at the window just as I fired up the engine. But I couldn't even make out if it was male or female.

"That was quick," I said.

"You were kipping."

"Was I?"

"Yes you fuckin' were. You're meant to be keepin' an eye on things."

"Thought I was just the driver."

I swung the Merc out into a sidestreet, and headed back south east.

"What's next?"

"Whitechapel."

Eventually, we hit the Stratford one-way system and went west over the Poplar fly-over towards the City.

Then I swung across the main road into a side street making him lurch across the back street.

"Take it fuckin' easy," he yelled.

"Still breathin' are you?" I said.

"Take a left up there," he mumbled.

We'd approached Whitechapel from the east, through a network of streets alongside abandoned warehouses and under loads of railway arches.

"Right here," said The Mole. We got to a narrow street that ran under yet another bridge which carried the new Docklands Light Railway. It was an area no-one spent much time in until a bunch of high flying City types started buying up the cheap housing in the mid-eighties, I guess.

It'd developed into a weird mix of pristine Victorian terraces, local shops, sleazy clubs and wine bars.

"Sling it up here," barked The Mole in his most charming voice.

A couple of minutes later we were walking into a club called The Surprise. But it wasn't the sort of place where you had a quiet half and a packet of dry roasted.

Girls in mini-skirts and tight leather and satin trousers were sitting at plastic tables spread out in front of a stage where a very young looking brunette was gyrating on the floor dressed in nothing but a pair of thigh hugging patent leather high-heeled boots and a nose stud.

A handful of businessmen types were sitting at the tables. Three slightly older women dressed head-to-toe in black rubber were leaning across the men taking their drinks orders.

"Charmin' little place." I said to The Mole. "D'you come here often?"

"Shut it!" he hissed at me as we walked up to the bar. I instantly noticed that three heavyset geezers seemed to recognise The Mole. But they took one look at me and kept their distance. I'm sure one of them was one of my old opponents from donkey's years back.

I kept quiet and watched all the flesh pressing going on a few feet in front of me. A lot of the girls seemed very young. That bothered me when I thought about Karen.

These kids were done up to the nines. Their faces covered in thick make-up, but I still recognised the slim, girlish figures of adolescents. I couldn't stop thinking about Karen.

I looked across at Jimmy The Mole to see what he was up to. He was leaning back against the bar taking a long look at two young blondes sitting and giggling at a table near the stage.

Eventually, one of them spotted us and started tottering towards us on her platforms. She was dressed in what looked like a school uniform. It was doing my head in, I can tell you. A girl disguised as a woman disguised as a child. It's bollocks, isn't it?

Just then The Mole barked at me: "Fuck this for a game of soldiers."

"What?"

"We're out of here!" he said turning towards the exit.

We hadn't even got as far as ordering a beer.

As we walked out I passed the same young girl who'd been coming towards us and she threw us a V-sign.

"Friend o' yours?" I asked.

The Mole didn't answer.

Couple of minutes later we were back in the Merc and he told me to head for Dalston. Eventually we reached a Victorian mansion block of flats in a tatty road.

"What now?"

"Drop us off here," he said.

"What 'bout tomorrow?" I asked.

"I'll be in touch."

I heard him fumbling through his wallet, and then he leaned forward and pushed some cash in my direction.

"Here. Get yourself a piece."

"What?"

"You're not much fuckin' use to me without a shooter."

"Leave it out. I don't touch 'em."

"Oh, yeah I nearly forgot. You're the fuckin' boss of all bosses. Skin of steel. Un-fuckin-killable."

"Leave it out," I said through gritted teeth.

He was shaking his head.

"There's more armed up fuckin' muscle merchants out there than you've had hot dinners."

But he still tried to push the bundle of readies into my hand. "Now take the fuckin' money."

"I don't carry shooters for no-one. End of story."

"You still think you're the hardest bastard in town don't you?"

I turned away from him.

He was shaking his head.

"Yeah. No one's gonna take a pop at The Boss are they?"

I still didn't respond.

"Just take the effin' dosh anyhow. Buy yourself a couple of gold plated knuckledusters." He forced the notes into my hand. "Goodnight."

Then he was gone, slamming the door behind him.

9

"Where ya got ta?" Carl asked, slapping eggs on to my plate.

I looked up from the book.

"I'm at the place where the caddy loses his memory and wakes up in a bunker with a gun in his hand."

"Ya got ta de bit where he finds de three-iron up another dead caddy's arse?"

"No."

"Ah," said Carl. "Da best is yet to come."

"It better come soon."

I tucked into the grub. Carl really knew how to make eggs melt in your mouth.

"So what's dis new job ya got?" he asked.

"Drivin'. That sorta thing."

"Drivin' wot?"

"My motor. Very demandin'."

"Who ya drivin'?"

"Some shortarsed toerag called Jimmy The Mole," I said.

"Wot's he up ta?"

"He's one of Benny's bloody milkmen."

"Ya sure?"

"I'm sure."

Carl laughed.

Then, I kind of let my old self-confidence get the better of me and I said: "Maybe I'll write a book about it all one day."

"I read dat one before."

I looked up from my food. "Yeah?"

"Fella com out o' de nick, looks up some people who owe him and gets a job drivin' de toerag round. But dis toerag, he treat driver like shit ..."

"How d'you know all that then?" I asked Carl.

"It's the way all dem stories start, man."

Just then my mobile started singing in my jacket.

"Dere he is," said Carl.

"Nah, he wouldn't be up yet," I said, wiping my mouth and pressing a greasy finger on the call button.

After a busy day, much of which was spent humping crates of illegal booze and fags around London, I found myself back in yet another sleazy boozer, twiddling with an empty packet of dry roasted and half of lager while The Mole leaned on some poor bastard for cash.

But, all things considered, I felt alright about things. During my lunch hour I'd blown some of The Mole's cash on a new suit. Getting myself decked out in some new clobber certainly put me in a better mood. Maybe I might even start being treated more like The Boss again.

Lapels had got narrower and three-pieces were no longer the rage. Even strides had lost their width over the previous twelve years, so I went for what I thought was up-to-date but not too flash.

I ended up with a well-fitted charcoal grey suit, rounding it off with a crisp white shirt and a pair of matt black, square-toed American loafers.

Despite the clobber, I got a right mouthful off Jimmy The Mole.

"Christ on a bike!" he had snorted at me when I picked him up earlier that evening.

"What d'you reckon?"

He shook his head.

"Pretty tasty, eh?" I continued.

"No wonder you won't use a shooter. You look like a fuckin' undertaker!" said The Mole.

I squeezed my fingers into the back pocket of the tightly fitted trousers, and pulled out some cash.

"Here's the change. You can take the rest outta my first week's salary," I said.

"Shut it," he said, almost pleasantly.

At the next pub The Mole marched past me after yet another conference with yet another manager and headed towards the door. Once we got out into the car park I saw a pissed off expression come across his face and thought he was going to start on me again.

"You're still famous," he said.

"What?"

"That lot back there were well fuckin' impressed to see The Boss back out in the real world."

"Wonderful," I said as low-key as possible.

"Maybe you're right ..." he said

"About what?"

"Maybe you don't need a shooter after all."

I didn't say another word and leaned across to unlock the passenger door for him from the inside. I couldn't tell if he was taking the piss or not — and he knew that. He knew that if I thought he was taking liberties, I'd give him a smack. That much was clear between us, but there was still a fucking unbearable atmosphere in the car. I knew I wouldn't be able to keep the lid on it for much longer.

It had all been a lot different 15 years earlier. In those days I had respect and a reputation as a decent brawler, well-known in pubs, clubs and sports halls right across the East End. Suppose I was a bit of a face, in some ways. But I didn't have to break any serious laws to get that respect. Just a few jaws.

Meanwhile, back in the modern, up-to-date world, an arsehole called Jimmy The Mole was paying me a wedge to hold his hand. In the old days this slimy little ratbag wouldn't have been fit to kiss my boots.

I started the engine of my motor and then let out a deep breath before reaching down into my pocket and pulling out a solid gold knuckleduster.

I fitted it around my right hand knuckles when we stopped at a set of traffic lights. Then I turned and smiled at him.

"This is the only weapon I need," I said.

"You're still living in the fucking past," responded The Mole. He sounded bored. He made me feel like I was a waste of space, and he did it on purpose.

I was spitting blood by this stage. With myself, with him, with my ruined life, with my family who didn't want to know me.

I whacked my foot down hard on the accelerator and turned into the street without bothering to check if anything was coming. The Mole didn't say a thing but I caught his eye every now and again in the rear view. He was glaring at me. Not only did he think I was some sort of washed-up has-been, now he thought I was bloody mental, too.

"You're right," I said. "In some ways I am livin' in the past. Can't help it. That's just the way I am."

"Being a failure is one thing," chipped in The Mole. "Thinkin' you're not really a failure takes talent."

"You take what you can in this life, don't you?"

"Yeah. And you got fuck all."

"Don't ever forget ..." I said through gritted teeth. "... I can still be a hard bastard when I want to be."

He didn't answer.

I reached forward and jammed the tape into the player. Papa Was A Rolling Stone. I flicked up the volume.

"For fuck's sake turn that shit off!" The Mole screamed.

"No."

Then I turned it up even louder before yelling over the music.

"You tried to make me buy a shooter. You shout orders at me what to do, where to go. No please. No thank you. Just do this, do that."

"Give it a fuckin' rest, will ya!"

That was it. I smacked the steering wheel with the palms of my hands and slammed the brakes on so hard we both almost went through the windscreen.

At least three cars behind me swerved to avoid hitting me. We were in the middle of the Angel one-way system. Hooters blared and a cabbie yelled abuse at me. I didn't give a toss.

"No one treats me like this," I screamed at him.

"Then fuck off!" The Mole shouted back.

That was it. My brain went AWOL. There was no turning back.

I smacked him so hard his head cracked back against the passenger door window. Then I marched round to his door, pulled it open and dragged him out and all the way up to the dog-shit infested grass verge on the traffic island in the middle of the one-way system.

All the time my music was still blaring away on the car stereo.

I pulled him to his feet and gave him a couple of right handers to jangle his brains a bit, then laid into him with one shot after another. He didn't put up any fight and I quickly realised that if I didn't get a grip of myself I would end up topping the bastard. A traffic jam of cars built up next to us. As yet another motorist blasted his horn the noise helped to bring me back to my senses.

The Mole was comatose on the grass. His half-open eyes stared up at the sky.

"Alright," I yelled down at him. "Now tell me to fuck off to my face."

His eyebrow was cut and bleeding, his cheeks starting to turn puffy and his mouth was swelling, with a trickle of blood running down his chin. Looked like I'd loosened a couple of teeth. But even through all the pain he still looked up at me with a nasty expression on his face.

"Fuck off, you wanker!" he spluttered. I've got to admit I admired his bottle.

"Magic. Best news I've had since I got my release papers."

I turned around and marched back towards the car.

As I was about to get in I turned and saw him struggling to sit up, his face screwed up with a mixture of pain and anger.

"Prick! You fuckin' twat! I'll have you some day," he screamed at me.

"Want some more of this?" I taunted him, flashing a fist in his direction. "Come on. Come and get it, you little shit."

In the old days I would have finished him off but I couldn't be bothered.

I got in the car, slammed the door and drove off. I glanced in my rear-view just as he was getting to his feet. I slowed the car down and craned my neck out of the window to have another look at him. He started walking in the opposite direction.

Fuck him. As the traffic started moving again I lost sight of him and decided the best thing to do was to find Carl and get tanked up.

I was just swinging into Dalston Lane when it dawned on me how fucking stupid I'd been. I'd just thrown away my only means of survival in the short term. What the hell was I doing?

I needed money to keep going. I needed it to try and win round Karen. Pride was the least important thing at that moment.

I thought about The Mole and realised I had no choice in the matter. I knew what I had to do. I swung the car around in a near-suicidal U-turn and headed back to Mile End.

The Mole wasn't difficult to find. He'd dragged his miserable carcass over the pedestrian barriers and was trying to get across the other side of the four-lane roundabout. He walked right across the road in front of me.

I swung the Merc over to the side of the road and jumped out.

He saw me at once, and backed off in the opposite direction, trying to hail a cab. Three went straight past him without stopping.

I chased after him and when I got close enough I shouted.

"We was both well out of order back there."

"Get fucked!"

"Look, I need this job. I can't get by without it."

"Should 'ave thought about that earlier."

"I just done a twelve stretch. It ain't easy adjusting."

"So?" said The Mole.

"So, I get a bit over sensitive sometimes."

I thought I caught a glimmer of sympathy in his face.

"My brief case still in the motor?" he said.

I nodded. We were alongside the car by now. He opened the front passenger door.

"You could at least get yourself a decent motor," he said.

Then he smiled. Luckily I hadn't done his face too much serious damage.

"Right, let's get this old heap on the road, then."

Back in the driving seat I said, "Where to?"

"Dog 'n' Duck on Darlston Road."

So I drove on.

There was no car park at The Dog 'n' Duck, so I had to wait in the motor while The Mole collected Benny Davies' milk money.

"Be about twenty minutes," said The Mole. "Look after all this lot for me."

He handed me a loose bundle of money. Dozens

and dozens of twenties and fifties.

"Bloody hell."

"I can't carry ten grand in there. Guard it with your life."

Then he was gone. I put all the notes into the glove compartment. Then I had second thoughts and decided to sit with it all back on my lap. Don't ask me why. I just wanted to keep an eye on it all.

When The Mole returned, he added more money to the pile.

"That's a good idea," he said. "Leave it out where everyone can see it."

I sighed and stuffed it all back in the glove compartment.

"What's next?" I asked.

"Loughton."

I looked over at him. "Oh."

"And get a move on. I'm runnin' late."

Half an hour later, I was parked on that gravel drive again drifting into a light doze. Just then I heard the sound of footsteps on the driveway and snapped awake. I didn't want another ear-bashing.

But it wasn't The Mole. It was some geezer wearing a white jacket like he was some kind of servant. As I came awake he lent down and started politely tapping on the window.

I wound it down.

"Thought you might like some refreshments, sir," he said, like a waiter in a posh hotel.

"Er ... right. I mean, er ... what you on about?"

"Tea and sandwiches."

"Yeah. Thanks," I said and took the tray he was offering.

"Um ... will he be long?" I asked.

"No more than usual, sir."

"Right."

I watched this bloke return to the house, and close the door. I balanced the tray on my knees, and switched on the interior light. The tea and milk were in silver pots: the cup and saucer were fancy china and the sandwiches were on a plate with a design in gold leaf.

I looked across at the house to make sure no one was watching me and took a sniff at the tea and peeled up a corner of the sarnie to see what was inside. Decent cuppa and chicken sandwiches. Well, well ...

I scoffed the lot down in a couple of minutes and even managed a second cup of tea.

As I finished it off I noticed lights coming on in the downstairs part of the house, so I brushed the crumbs off my lap and checked myself in the rear-view mirror. Then there was the tea tray. I couldn't take it with me and I certainly couldn't dump it on the drive.

I got out and arrived at the front door just as it opened. The Mole was there, clad in his grey overcoat and looking a bit rough and ready around the face where I had knocked him about. He looked pretty pissed off to see me standing there. Beside him was a man I'd never seen before. He was short and greasy looking with a shiny long black hair and a little goatee beard.

They both stared at me.

I broke the silence. "Sorry. I, er, didn't know what to do with the tray."

"I'll take it," the goatee geezer said. I didn't like the way he was smiling at me.

So I gave it to him and wondered where the servant in the white jacket had got to. I tried to see past him, but then The Mole grabbed my arm and wheeled me around.

Without even looking behind him once he walked me back to the Merc.

A few minutes later we were driving down the Balls Pond Road when I asked him: "Is he the main man, then?"

He ignored me, so I carried on.

"Took his time this evening."

The Mole didn't respond, again.

"Sorry ..." I said, and I meant it, "... you know what a nosy bastard I am."

"At least now you fuckin' know you are."

I shook my head and changed the subject.

"Where to now?"

"Whitechapel."

"Back to The Surprise?"

He ignored me and produced a cigarette. I pressed the dashboard cigar lighter.

"Ta," said The Mole.

The lighter popped out and he lit his fag before taking in a long deep breath of smoke. Then he wound down the window a couple of inches and blew it out into the street. As we moved rapidly west he gazed out of the window, watching the green and leafy streets of Loughton give way to the shabby shop fronts of Chingford.

"Jesus, they're young!" I said.

"Yeah, and most of them won't even get to middle age."

Jimmy The Mole sounded odd, as if he was talking but not listening to his own words. He was leaning against the bar in The Surprise, watching the girls giggling and dancing for individual tables just ten feet away from us.

"Tell me somethin'?" I asked.

"What?"

"Why don't any of them come near us?"

"What?"

"They're always givin' us a wide berth."

The Mole just drew on his fag and blew out another stream of smoke. He was watching a young, blonde, Slavic-looking girl move gracefully round the tables to where two young business types were sitting. She was a real looker but, like the rest of the girls, she couldn't have been much older than my Karen. That thought really dragged me down.

"The girls know who you are, right?" I asked.

"Maybe," he paused, as if his attention had been diverted by something he'd seen.

I got the message and stopped rabbiting.

In the dim light of the club most of the girls

looked young and fragile, and the one in front of us had an awkward, young girl's tilt as she leaned down to talk to the two businessmen.

Then an older woman in her mid-thirties, dressed in a rubber catsuit and heels so high her arse had climbed half-way up her back, walked past us looking straight at The Mole. He turned away and took a swig of his whisky.

A swarthy-looking Latin — or he might have been an Arab — went up to the younger Slavic blonde girl and she broke away from the two blokes to talk to him. This guy put an arm around her shoulder.

"She doesn't hang about, does she?" I said.

"Pratt!" The Mole whispered. "That's her pimp."

I cracked my knuckles and felt a bit of a dickhead for not knowing the rules of the game in The Surprise.

"Time to go," said The Mole.

I was mightily relieved to pull the motor out of there and head towards the Mile End Road.

Eventually I felt obliged to ask The Mole: "So what's it all about? You don't collect no payments when you go into that place. What's the story here?"

"Somethin' very fuckin' personal."

"I'm just curious."

"Curiosity killed the fuckin' cat," pointed out Jimmy The Mole.

By that time I'd reached the traffic lights just ahead of the Mile End one-way system.

"Left or right?"

"Right," he ran a finger over his swollen lip.

"Please."

We drove off up towards Dalston. Another's night's work in the bag, thank God.

10

For twelve years I got up at 6 a.m. every day in my capacity as an inmate of Her Majesty's Prisons. It always seemed to be bloody freezing and I was usually so knackered by lunchtime my brain was about as much use as a damp fucking sock. So when I got out I promised myself I'd get a few late starts under my belt.

It was Saturday so I knew I could get a lie-in, tucked up in the narrow spare bed at Carl's place. By the time I got up I found Carl down at the workbench in his lock-up.

"Any brekkie on the go?" I asked.

"Breakfast was three hours back, man. Hang around a bit an' lunch might appear."

"What you up to?" I asked.

"Burglar alarms."

"Don't they work?"

"When ya got hot product ya gotta know how ta sell it." Carl carried on fiddling with a screw-driver. "By the way, ya mobile keeps ringin'."

"It's Saturday ... my day off."

"Dat's wot I taught, so I didn't wake ya."

Then he added: "It might be him."

"Who?"

"De Mole Man?"

"That's evening work only."

Then my phone went again. Carl was right. It was The Mole. That evening I was to take him to the same hotel in the Docklands where I'd met him the first night. I was starting to think that I might be just as well picking up fares for Carl's mini cab business. Mind you, The Mole paid better, and he was still my best bet for getting hold of Benny again.

11

A few hours later, decked out in my flash new suit, I found myself driving The Mole down the Vallance Road, where the Kray twins lived when they was running the manor more than thirty years back.

The second we got to the hotel in the Docklands, the Mole jumped out the Merc and hurried across the car park towards the hotel's revolving doors.

I struggled to keep up with him.

We passed the doorman, and went through the swinging double doors into the saloon bar.

He told me to get a drink and wait. Then he turned and headed for the lifts. There wasn't a hint of what he was up to.

The waiter with the ponytail was watching me. I

was going to have a word with the stupid git about his bloody stupid haircut, then I thought better of it and went off to find a table.

"The usual, sir?" he followed me to the table.

"Usual? How many times I been here?"

"Bottle of lager, isn't it?"

"Well done."

I was starting to feel more at home. Maybe it was the clothes. I was getting a bit of the respect I thought I deserved. I didn't feel like a pork sausage in a synagogue no more. Even the waiter was starting to seem like a decent enough bloke. Noticed he had an earring, though, and I've always had them marked down for either pirates or poofters.

I took two swift gulps of my lager and glanced across at the reception area, looking for The Mole. That's when I noticed one of the function rooms on the first floor that overlooked the lobby area was in use. The double doors were open and one of the hotel staff, dressed in a DJ, was checking the invitations of all those going in.

Lots of people were milling about on the landing, some of them had spilled out from the party inside.

One of the guests was Benny Davies, the man who'd got me sent down. The man who once promised to make me the richest fighter in East London.

I dumped my drink and moved quickly across the lobby. I took the stairs two at a time and headed straight for the double doors as Benny was moving inside.

"Your invitation, sir?"

The waiter was blocking my way firmly, but politely.

"Gotta see someone," I said, trying to look over his shoulder at the throng of people inside.

"Of course you have, sir. But I need to see your invitation first."

Just then I spotted Benny just a few yards in front of me.

"Benny!" I yelled. "Benny!"

I forced my way past the geezer at the door, and shouted Benny's name again. Behind me, someone was trying to pull me back by tugging on my new suit jacket.

At that moment Benny spotted me. He immediately broke off from his conversation, and headed straight towards me.

"Bloody hell, Tony!"

With Benny gently pushing me and the hotel man pulling me, they got me out onto the landing in seconds. I smiled at Benny. Thought he'd be pleased to see me.

"Bet you're wondering what I'm doin' here," I said.

"Not at all, Tone," Benny muttered under his breath.

"So here I am."

"Good to see you, Tone, my old son." Benny was looking straight at me nodding his head slowly, already backing away from me.

"Benny, we gotta talk ..."

"Bit tied up at the moment, Tony. But ..."

"Come on, Benny. It won't take long," I said.

I suddenly became aware that someone else was

hovering behind me. Then I noticed Benny's eyes looking in this person's direction.

"I'll call you, Tony."

"Leave it out, Benny. You never call no one."

Benny looked back at the man standing behind him, and I suddenly realised who that man was. It was that same little geezer with the goatee from the house in Loughton.

Benny turned his back on me and muttered something to this fellow, who smiled in agreement and walked calmly back into the main party. No one asked to see his fucking invitation.

Then Benny said to me: "Come on, Tone, you can see I'm busy."

"Yeah. But I been trying to get hold of you ..."

"... I thought Henry was lookin' after you."

"He did, but ... it's been twelve bloody years, Benny ..."

"Not now, Tone."

"We gotta talk, Benny," I said.

"Sure we have, old son. I'll bell you soon as I can."

"That a promise?"

"Would I let you down?"

He winked broadly at me, raised a hand, and waved me away. I did the same back even though I knew he'd never call me.

"You sure, Benny?"

"I promise, Tone ..."

Then he was gone. I stared after him, through the double doors and into the milling crowd of people, knowing that Benny was still trying to take me for a mug.

Two halves of lager later, The Mole reappeared.

Naturally, I asked him about Benny.

"Did you know Benny was here?" I said.

"I been upstairs at a meet, Tony. Dunno what you're on about."

I don't know why but I decided to drop the subject and off we went.

Half a dozen pub visits later, The Mole and I were back at The Surprise Club, in Whitechapel.

"What's goin' on?" I asked.

"What?"

"All this."

"It's not what you think."

He sounded angry.

Funny thing is, I believed him.

I stared ahead looking at the girls swinging their hips between the tables full of businessmen. One girl turned and looked in our direction.

"I got a daughter her age," I said.

"They're all somebody's daughters, Tony."

The one I'd spotted started tottering on her heels towards us. The Mole said nothing, his eyes stared ahead into space.

The young girl came right up to me. She slid in front of me and her loose black see-through blouse hung open to reveal tiny breasts.

"You want me to dance for you?" she said, before taking a long sniff. She was chewing hard on some gum. I could see it each time her mouth opened.

"Not tonight, thanks," I mumbled. I looked dead ahead as I spoke to her. I was embarrassed. The Mole remained alongside me, saying nothing.

"You wanna go somewhere later?" the girl said. "I do whatever you want ..." Then she looked across at the Mole. "I do you and your friend ... it's no problem."

"No, thanks," I said.

Then she leaned forward, rubbing herself against me and whispered in my ear.

"Don't you like me?" She hissed. Then she slid her hand below my waist and squeezed hard.

Still leaning into me, the girl whispered, "You want it. All men want it."

"No, thanks," I said, trying to remove her hand.

She brought her face even closer to mine. Then she leaned back and looked into my eyes. I could feel the hate burning into me as I grabbed her wrist tightly and forced her hand away.

That's when she spat at me.

Then she turned and walked away, glancing across the bar at a black guy who was staring right at us. I guessed he was her pimp.

He immediately moved alongside me.

His face was level with mine. I could smell his shitty dog's breath. Nicotine. Booze. Burgers. I stared straight ahead, wishing I was somewhere else.

"Yo not pay de girls yo' fuckin' get outta here, man. I see ya again I kick yo' and yo' friend. Ya dig?"

As you all know by now, I don't like being leaned on by anyone. I turned to face the pimp. He was wearing a flashy, purple velvet shell suit. I knew I'd only get one good crack at him.

"Yo' dig?" the pimp asked again. Then he glanced across at The Mole. "And I told yo' before that I can't help you."

"Come on, let's go," The Mole said to me.

But I was so fuckin' furious by this stage that his words just didn't sink in.

Then the pimp spat out more abuse: "If Anif find out yo' back here he gonna shoot ya in de face. Ya dig?"

"Move it!" The Mole hissed at me.

But I wanted a face-off with this bastard.

"He gonna 'ave yo'. Ya dig?"

"Fuckin' shut it!" I yelled at this piece of shit. Now I knew there was going to be a ruck and there didn't seem much point in avoiding it. Now I wanted it.

It's difficult to put these feelings of violence into words.

It's like a stabbing feeling in the bottom of my belly, and it goes right up through me. It makes me feel hot, sweaty. It makes me feel strong — strong enough to sort out anyone. Suppose it's hatred, that's what it is, hatred. Pure fucking hatred.

At that moment if you said to me I could kill the man I was eyeballing and there would be no comeback, then I would do it. It wouldn't bother me. If it was a matter of him or me then I'd settle for being the one who kills. When I get angry, it all comes rushing out.

My penchant for violence had an outlet during my days in the ring and those bare-knuckle barneys inside. But at heart I'm a street fighter, a pub scrapper who found a way to trade on his inner anger and torment. But that doesn't stop my brand of violence being other people's real-life nightmare. When those feelings kick in I'm capable of anything.

If someone crosses me or my friends or family, my brain short-circuits. I get like a madman. I don't need a shooter, and I couldn't give a fuck about the consequences of what I'm about to do.

That's what was happeneing as I stood there in The Surprise Club that night. My eyes were getting wild. Anyone challenging me would have to be off his fucking head. I could feel my body twitching and straining. I was ready for this bastard.

My hands snapped out and grabbed the pimp's head and I smashed his jaw down on the corner of the bar. There was a cracking sound and I knew I had hurt him, so I did it again and again. Each time harder. Bits of his teeth and blood were flying everywhere. Then I gave him a right uppercut in the face. His nose exploded. Then I let go. He fell to the ground.

"Now look what you made me do," I said, as the pimp scrambled around holding his face in his hands on the floor, crumpled up and expecting a good kicking.

The Mole yelled at me. "For fuck's sake let's get outta here!"

This time I did as I was told. I strode up the stairs past two doormen who thought better of trying to challenge me. Two girls scurried out of the way to avoid us.

As I got onto the pavement, I turned to see the pimp

slowly trying to climb the stairs after us. No one seemed to want to help him.

We jumped in the Merc and I didn't take my foot off the gas until we got to the Caledonian Road. Then I muttered under my breath; "Jesus H Christ."

The Mole was somewhere alongside me. I turned my head to check him out. He was leaning against the passenger door window, looking shaken.

"What the fuck is your game?" I said.

"It's no game, Tony."

"Then what the bloody hell are you into? That cunt was ready to turn the dogs on us before I gave him a pastin'— and he knew exactly who you were. So what's the fuckin' story here?"

12

A few minutes later I pulled the Merc up outside The Mole's block of flats, and switched off the engine. My right hand was throbbing, so I flicked on the interior light and examined it. My knuckles were bruised and two of them were bleeding. Some of the blood had seeped onto the cuff of my new shirt and jacket. Pity, but a bit of cold water would sort that out.

"He got what he deserved," I said, nursing my hand.

"Yeah and I'm sure he'll be told exactly who hit him," The Mole said alongside me.

"So, what's this all about?"

The Mole let out a soft sigh.

"It doesn't matter."

"I doesn't matter?" I said. "I just battered some geezer senseless and you're saying it doesn't matter?" I paused again. "I've got a right to know."

"It's personal."

"I couldn't give a fuck what it is. I just want to know what I've got myself into here."

"Not here. Come up."

He got out of the car and began walking towards the main entrance. I looked up and followed him.

The main door was protected by a double lock and an entry phone. But the hall inside was surprisingly bare. It led to a corridor and then a lift with a mesh gate. Concrete stairs spiralled around the lift shaft. The Mole punched the button for the ninth floor.

There was a lurch and we started going up slowly. I watched each of the landings go past. Someone had painted the number of every floor on the concrete sill as the lift approached that level.

I counted them off to myself, one by one.

The Mole's flat was at the far end of the corridor and was protected by a double lock. He led me into a living room that seemed reasonably decorated. It didn't look like he'd lived there long. There were no pictures on the wall but he'd certainly spent a few bob on the furniture. Not a bad gaff at all.

He put his briefcase down and then opened one of the windows to let in some fresh air.

"You need to get that sorted," he said, looking at my hand. "There's plenty of stuff in the bathroom. Help yourself."

He nodded towards the hallway.

I wandered off as he leaned down to turn on the telly.

I rustled up some bandage and cotton wool. The Mole went through to the kitchen and came back with a bowl of warm water, a cloth and a small sponge.

I took it from him.

"Looks nasty," he said.

"I've had worse."

"S'ppose you must 'ave."

I dabbed at my own hand and cleaned out the graze. Then, using the sponge, I dabbed at the bloodstains on my clothes.

"That scumbag knew you," I said.

"Yeah. It's a long story."

I pushed aside the bowl and the sponge.

"I've got all night."

The Mole shifted nervously on a chair in front of me.

I was getting impatient. But for the first time since we'd met I felt more in control of the situation than he was.

"Well?"

"I've had dealings with him in the past."

"Dealings? What sort of dealings?"

"He threatened to cut me up a few times."

"Why?"

The Mole moved position again, looking extremely uncomfortable. "I've got this daughter, like. She's a lovely kid. But she's got a habit. Kept gettin' into trouble. Then she got caught up on the game."

"Jesus. I'm sorry," I said. And I really meant it.

Then came one of those awkward silences that feels like a sheet of steel has dropped down between you and whoever it is you're talking to. I've never been much good at talking my way around things like that and was thinking about buggering off home when The Mole turned towards me.

"She's got a serious problem ..."

All The Mole could see at that moment was his beloved daughter high on smack.

"... I'm talkin' about the sort of habit where you stick needles in your arm. Her bastard pimp got her onto that shit ..." he paused, "... he hooked her in."

Another awkward silence followed. The Mole got up, went to a drinks cabinet on the other side of the room and came back with two glasses of neat scotch.

Then he went on.

"... I tried to get her back. But each time she'd stay a few days then do a runner. One day I just stopped tryin'."

He paused yet again.

"Me and my missus just couldn't deal with it. She blamed me. I blamed her. You see Jenny, that's her name, was our only kid. We put all our love and care into her. Spoilt her rotten we did.

"Anyhow, few months after Jenny went walkabout for the last time me and the missus split up. We couldn't handle our lovely little baby turning into a smack head."

He took a long gulp of scotch, knocking back half the contents of his glass.

"I went off to Spain and did some collectin' and

stuff from a few of the firms' outlets down round Marbella. Then about six months back my missus went and did herself in. What a waste of a life. Most of it was down to me and all the rowing about our kid.

"I came back to London and rented this place. That's why I started doing the milk rounds for Benny. I had to get myself back on Jenny's old patch just in case she showed up.

"The Surprise is the only place I know where she might turn up. I often see some of her mates in the club and I'm sure some of the girls know where Jenny is."

He reached behind him and pulled a photo album out from a pile of books on the floor under a chair. It opened at two pages of Polaroid pictures.

She was young and frail looking, with thin features and straw-coloured hair. She was dressed in a baggy anorak and a woollen hat but I could see she had that same angry teenage look on her face as my own daughter Karen. It sent a shiver up my spine.

"She's got a tattoo on her right hand ... like this ..."

He drew a small heart with his fingertip on the back of his hand.

"... it's small and blue, with a smaller one inside."

I stared at the photos for at least a couple of minutes, thinking how it could so easily have been my Karen. They might have been sisters.

"I gotta track her down," The Mole said. "Anythin' can happen out there on the streets, in the clubs. I can't lose her as well as my missus."

He paused and looked up at me.

"I'll pay you to find her."

"What?"

"I can't keep going down there. They all know who I am. But you could track her down."

"What?"

"I gotta find her. You're a dad. You know how I feel."

"'Course I do," I said, wondering if he really meant what he was saying. "But I'm twelve years out of date. I don't even know who's running things no more."

"Exactly. You stand a chance."

"Look, I know how you must feel but ..."

"You're a decent fellow, Tony."

"What makes you think that?"

"I know."

I paused and took a few seconds to consider his proposition.

Then The Mole added, "I'll pay you well."

"Fuck the money. But I'll do it."

"You sure?"

"You just want me to find her. Right?"

"I want to know she's okay."

He took the album from me and closed it.

Then he got up and said he was going to bed. A few minutes later, I put down my empty glass and let myself out of his front door.

I wondered if I'd just made the biggest mistake of my life.

On my way back to Carl's place, I took a detour and thought about going to The Surprise again. Then I remembered that I'd get nothing but a kicking if I dropped in there so soon after the spot of bother earlier that evening.

So I drove cautiously along the same old road under the bridge near the club, wondering if Jenny or her pimp might walk by, or something.

But it was late now, and most of the girls had gone. I saw two pros still on patrol, standing together in the cone of amber light underneath a lamp post.

As my headlights picked them out they both looked up expectantly. Their faces reminded me of what drowned swimmers look like, only these girls was sinking in a sea of sleaze.

What a fucked-up world I'd move back into.

13

I thought Carl was either asleep or over at one of his birds' places when I crept back into the flat. But as I moved through the living room area he appeared in a doorway.

"Tone?"

"Yup," I said.

Carl stood there looking at me for a few seconds. He knew something was wrong.

"G'night, Carl," I said.

"Wot's up, my friend."

"This an' that."

"Like wot?"

I took a deep breath.

"Gotta lot on my plate, Carl."

Carl looked my new clobber up and down.

"Flash new gear," he shook his head slowly. "Yo' locked yo'self in, my friend. Yo' joined de firm."

"No, I ain't."

"Look like it ta me."

My hand was hurting, and my mind was foggy.

I looked at Carl and shrugged my shoulders.

"Gotta sort myself out, Carl."

"Taught yo' already 'ad."

"Nah, I mean my life. There's gotta be something else out there."

"Told yo'. Tings 'ave changed."

"Yeah. But I gotta survive."

"Survive on yo' own, my friend. Yo don't need dere help."

"You may be right. But first I gotta sort out one big problem."

"Wot sorta problem?" he asked.

Then I told Carl all about The Mole's daughter Jenny.

After I'd finished he still had the same expression on his face. Now I'm not one for explaining my actions to anyone. But Carl's not just anyone.

"Look, all I said was I'd help him," I told Carl. "His daughter's gone awol. She's young, on the game. I know what she looks like. You'd do the same."

"Wot's in it fa ya?" asked Carl.

"That's not the point," I replied. "It could easily be one of our kids out there."

"Dat why yo' doin' it?"

"What d'you mean?"

"Yo' feelin' guilty 'bout your kid so you help diss fella to find 'is daughter?"

"Maybe ..."

"Wot yo' goin' ta da? Go up ta doormen in clubs and say, 'Hello, I'm lookin' for a hooker.'"

I stopped and let his words sink in for a few moments.

"She might 'ave gone off the game and be doin' something else. She could be anywhere. But I gotta give it a go."

"I s'ppose," said Carl.

I had to do two return trips to Tilbury on booze and fags business which took me most of Monday morning. In the afternoon I had an hour or two to kill so I parked the Merc up just off the Bow Road and went for a stroll.

I headed up toward Pudding Mill Lane and into one of about half a dozen side streets where a lot of the East Ends' most notorious clip joints are located. First place I came across seemed as good a place to start as any.

Two geezers standing at the door looked a bit bothered the moment I approached them.

"What sorta girls you got in here?" I asked. Suppose I should have known better.

"Every colour you want," one of them said in a heavy foreign accent.

The sign TOPLESS BAR was fluttering on and off. Sort of place that probably hadn't changed much in 25 years.

I moved towards the entrance and one of these geezers immediately blocked my way.

"That'll be a tenner, pal."

"A tenner, just to walk through a door?"

"It's a club. You gotta join."

Muttering under my breath I pulled out a tenner and handed it over. All I got was a pink ticket with a number on it in return. The same sort of ticket I used to get in the church fete raffle when I was a kid.

I shouldered my way past them and started down some creaky black wooden stairs.

I was surprised by the decor. It was almost classy. The tables had cloths on them. Dark red velvet curtains lined the walls and lamps with green shades gave it a low-key atmosphere. But it still smelt like all the rest of these places I'd been in.

Three or four girls sat in a group in one booth in the far corner. As I walked in they all looked up.

I ignored them and headed for the bar. A young girl with masses of jet black curly hair was wiping up the glasses.

I looked at her chest and said: "I thought this was a topless bar."

"After six. That's the rules."

"You should say that on the door."

"You want a drink, or what?"

I'd heard all this bollocks before. I glanced around and felt bloody depressed by it all.

"What d'you want to drink?" she repeated impatiently.

"Nothin' thanks."

"You buy a ticket then you buy a drink. That's the rules."

"How much?"

"Twelve pounds minimum."

"Don't tell me, that's the rules?"

"You want to meet a girl, you have to buy a drink."

I glanced back at the table. There were no blondes to be seen.

"Look ... before I buy a drink, will you tell me one thing?"

"What?"

"You got any blonde girls here?"

The girl smiled like she was delighted I'd asked.

"Sure we have."

She reached up, and pulled at her hair. The black wig came away, revealing a boyish, elfin head of blonde close-cropped hair. She was transformed.

"What d'you reckon?"

I found another strip club just round the corner, pulled out another tenner and went down into yet another cellar. Some bird in jackbboots and a Nazi helmet was strutting away with a bottle of baby oil on a tiny stage. Techno music, I'm reliably informed that that's what they call this shit, was blaring away and five or six fat, sweaty business types were drooling at her. Sad bastards.

I stood at the back for a minute or two, then noticed a door marked 'No Entry'. I wandered over, opened it, and squeezed along a narrow corridor.

That fucking awful music was even louder here.

Eventually, I got to a small alcove crammed with costumes. There was a young girl amongst them, frantically looking through them like she'd lost her best Sunday school frock. Although somehow I doubt if that was the case. At first all I could see were the pimples on her back and shoulder blades, but when she turned around she had a cup of tea in front of her, and not much else.

She looked up at me: "Who the hell are you?"

I smiled. "Any chance of a cuppa?"

"Piss off."

"Don't be like that ... I didn't get any lunch."

I backed away. I could see out through the back onto the stage where a flat-chested Chinese girl was now swinging round a flimsy looking dance pole.

Behind me, the girl in amongst the costumes said: "You better get out or I'm callin' the management."

"I'm on my way."

I walked straight out with no intention of ever going back.

Next stop was a peep show in a converted shop near where I'd delivered some booze and fags a few days earlier.

I'd never been to a peep show in my life and when I entered the shop I was curious to know what it was all about. I quickly wished I hadn't bothered.

I approached a dopey looking punk girl in a black PVC t-shirt on the desk. She was busy counting out £1 coins and occasionally filing her jet black fingernails.

"It's alright. I already got a pocketful of them."

"You have to change them here. Rules."

"All right ... how much?"

"Minimum of ten pounds."

I handed over a tenner, and was given nine coins in return.

"And the rest," I said.

"That's the membership fee."

"Those rules ... they don't say anything about six o'clock do they?"

The girl looked at me a bit odd and I went on through. Beyond the next door was the peep show itself: a group of curtained booths clustered around a metal box inside which the 'artiste' performed.

I found an empty booth and slipped two £1 coins into the slot. A metal shutter flipped open, just below comfortable eye level, and I leaned forward to see what was happening.

The interior of the peep show was lit by two bare light bulbs. A tacky-looking speaker was stuck on the wall next to me and music was crackling out of it. Two naked girls gyrated with blank looks on their faces. Each of them was performing to the circle of slits on the walls that surrounded them. Some of them were open with hungry eyes visible behind them. Then the shutters closed down with a thud as the money ran out.

My arrival didn't exactly cause much of a stir. One of the girls moved over to my eye slit, wiggled her tits a couple of times and then raised a leg to give me a close-up view. It wasn't pleasant.

Just then my shutter closed and a tinny sounding male voice on the loud speaker in my cubicle announced that a blonde called Sammy was on next. "She's got a very big surprise in store for you."

I reluctantly reached for two more coins to push in the slot because there was just a slim chance Sammy might be the girl I was looking for. Yeah, I know what you're thinking, sounds like a pretty feeble excuse, but believe me, this place was such a shithole I wouldn't have stayed a second longer than I had to.

Moments after putting the money in, the shutter snapped open and all I could see were what I presumed was Sammy's very big suprise — a very firm, uplifting pair of silicone-filled boobs swinging around about two feet from my face. The girl then stood up to expose more of her body.

For a split second I couldn't believe my eyes. 'She' was a fella and she had her meat and two veg pointed right in my direction. I sat back with a jolt and felt the bile rising up through my throat. I'd never seen anything like it in my whole bloody life.

As I backed out of the cubicle I trod on a sea of screwed up bits of tissue paper and newspaper. It was bloody disgusting.

Around the back of the peep show box was a door with PRIVATE written on it. Beyond that was a plastic beaded curtain. I walked through.

Four girls were sitting in a smelly, smoke-filled room. They were waiting their turn, wearing robes, housecoats and over-the-top make-up. None of them looked up.

"Fuck off," one of them hissed. Her voice was so deep it might have been another fella.

"I'm looking for someone," I said.

The girl nearest put down her newspaper and looked me up and down.

"Aren't we all?"

"Yeah," I said hopefully. "Her name's Jenny ..."

"Just get outta here."

But I ignored her.

"... her name's Jenny, she's got blonde hair and a blue tatoo on one hand."

I delivered the words as quickly as possible knowing I only had a matter of seconds left.

"Fuck off," shouted the ringleader.

"Stick another two quid in the slot and have a wank, handsome," said one girl.

"Only askin'," I said, feeling like a right plonker in the process.

I backed out of the room and returned to the main area where some fellow was squirting water on the walls with a pressure pump. As I stood there he splashed a lot of it over me. I ducked and raised an arm.

"Oi! Leave it out!"

"Sorry, guv." He lowered the nozzle then looked at me for a moment. "Don't I know you?"

"Do you?" I replied, not in the least bit curious about who he was.

"Blimey, Tony Mills! The Boss. Saw you demolish Eddie The Hammer Jones at the Stepney Dome."

I looked him up and down. Yeah, I remembered

him. Kenny something-or-other. I was buggered if I could remember his second name. Like as not I had never known it anyway.

"Kenny, how's it goin'? What you doin' in this dump?"

"Gotta earn a livin'."

"You worked here long?"

"Couple o' months," he hesitated. "Just finished a three-stretch."

I didn't bother asking what for. I had other things on my mind.

"I'm tryin' to find a bird, Kenny. Can you help?"

"What sorta bird?"

"Well, I met this young one, on the hustle a couple of days back. Nice girl called Jenny."

"And?"

"She works in a club round here, but I was so pissed up when I met her I forgot which one it was."

"What's she look like?"

"Spiky hair, blonde. Not spiky like the bird out there on the deck, but sort of short on top."

Kenny looked across at me and scratched his chin with a thoughtful expression on his face.

"You could be in luck, Tony old son."

"D'you know who I mean? She's got a tattoo."

"On her arse, ain't it?"

"Nah. Back of her hand. Two hearts, one inside the other."

Kenny nodded his head in recognition. "Come back here in an hour, Tony. Might be able to help you."

"I can't make it, then. I gotta work."

"Later this evening, then."

I thought about it, knowing there were long gaps in the night when all I had to do was sit in the motor or at a bar waiting for the The Mole to finish his business.

"Alright, Where?"

"The Go-Go on Devons Road. Make sure you're there."

"What time?"

"Whatever time you like, Tony."

14

That night it bucketed down with rain and then a thick mist descended on the East End. That just about summed up the state of my brain as I ferried The Mole round his usual haunts. I wished I didn't get so wound up by everything I did. I wished I could be more laid back, a bit like Benny Davies had been in the old days.

Back then he'd risen to become one of the most powerful figures in the local fight game because he'd always been the coolest customer of all. Nothing bothered him and that's why he copped a small fortune promoting some of the most one-sided contests in the history of bare knuckle, as well as legit, fights.

One time he arranged a tournament pitching some

of the Old Bill's finest homegrown scrappers up agaianst a bunch of local talent. Benny was so artful he deliberately put up some complete no-hopers so that The Filth won every bout. Benny knew what side his bread was buttered on.

"Just keep a low profile, take home some decent wedge and lead a quiet, normal life," he'd say to me back then.

Meanwhile in the East End fog, The Mole had just jumped back in the Merc after yet another visit on his milkround and I'd decided I needed someone to talk to.

"Don't you ever want to walk away from all this bollocks?"

"What?"

"This fuckin' business."

"It's all I got, ain't it?" The Mole said.

"But it'd be easy to pack it all in, surely?"

"You reckon?"

The Mole laughed which made me turn and look him in the face.

"... we're in it up to our necks, old son," he said cheerfully. "... up to our fuckin' necks. It's the only way. What are you goin' to do if you're not on the team? Stack fuckin' shelves in Asda?"

He had a point, but I didn't agree entirely. I still had a notion to find myself a legit way to earn a living. I drove slowly and carefully that evening. I was feeling as if I didn't really want to be there.

Eventually we arrived at The George, one of the biggest pubs in Canning Town.

We were walking across the tarmac towards the pub itself — a few feet from the main doors — when we both noticed someone standing just inside the lobby area. He was a heavy-looking, thick-necked geezer eyeballing us through the glass doors. As we approached he moved back next to a fruit machine.

The Mole glanced over at me and said: "He looks like a hired hand."

"What's he up to?" I asked.

"The landlord may be about to blow us out, so he's called in a bit of personal protection. Happens all the time."

"Yeah?"

"Keep an eye on him for me."

"Right."

I nodded.

As we walked towards the main bar, the same Muppet with the thick neck glanced at us in a funny sort of way. I swung the doors open. The Mole went first, then I followed.

I was sure I'd seen this geezer somewhere before. Maybe it was in the nick? It bothered me big time that I couldn't put a name to his face.

As we walked through the main saloon bar it felt like everyone's eyes were on us. Something was up. No doubt about it.

Then, as was always customary in this particular boozer, we waited at the main bar for a couple of minutes. The familiar-looking face plonked himself in a seat at the far end of the bar, looking straight at us with a nasty expression.

Then one of the barmen appeared and gave The Mole the nod to go upstairs. Usually, I'd stay in the bar but this time The Mole gestured for me to follow him, so I moved behind the bar and towards some stairs.

Neither of us said anything but we both kept our eyes well peeled.

When we got to the top of the stairs, a long, blood red coloured corridor stretched away on either side. My eyes snapped in all directions to see if anyone was around. Not a soul.

As we approached the door to the pub landlord's office, The Mole added.

"Trouble with this game is it makes you fuckin' paranoid," Jimmy The Mole said finally.

"There's nothin' happenin' here. You can pull out if you want."

"You sure?"

"Yeah."

"Want me to wait downstairs?"

"I'll be at least an hour. Me and this fella got some serious talkin' to do.

Yet again I found myself wondering what the hell I was doing involved in a bloody milk round. Carl was right. If I didn't make some new, legitimate, plans quickly then I'd be sucked into all this dodgy shit for the rest of my life.

And that would probably end in another long stretch inside.

I left the Merc at the pub and grabbed a cab to

Devons Road. I hadn't mentioned anything to The Mole about Kenny's promise to find me the girl because I didn't want to get his hopes up too high. I knew he'd bloody kill me if I wasn't waiting in the car for him. I'd just have to make sure I was back within the hour.

The Go-Go Club was in a narrow lane just off Devons Road. I swept past the bouncers on the door but this time they didn't seem to give a toss.

Kenny was sitting there, dressed in a tacky checked suit with three girls crowding round him. When he saw me he got up and wandered over.

"Well," I said. "Any joy?"

"Did my best."

"What's that mean?"

"You sure 'bout this, Tony?"

"Why?"

"She's young. Very young."

I ignored him for a moment then asked him awkwardly, "How d'you know she's the right one?"

"Jenny ... her name's Jenny. She's got the tatt and everythin' you was after ..."

He looked away from me as he spoke.

"... I'm a bit busy at the moment ..." he nodded in the direction of his girlie friends. "... so Ian will take you to her."

"Who the hell's Ian?"

"He's alright, Tone."

He could tell I wasn't impressed and he knew me well enough to know that he was only a grunt away from having his head shoved up his arse.

"Wait here, mate," he said. "I'll go an' sort it out for you."

Kenny then went out the door, and came back two minutes later with one of the gorillas from outside. I presumed this was Ian.

This geezer immediately jerked his head, meaning that I had to follow him. Without saying a word he started led me to a door alongside the club's front entrance and up two flights of stairs.

Half way up Ian suddenly remembers he can speak and tells me: "Kenny says you're alright so you can pay up afterwards."

"Thanks," I said, although I know it came out sounding like, "Big fuckin' deal."

Then we got to a door.

"You got twenty minutes."

"All right, all right. I can tell the time."

"And don't damage the goods 'cause her fella is a right nutter."

"That's not my style," I said coldly.

Then I turned and went into the room.

15

A young girl was lying on a bed with a tatty pale green towel laid out over the covers. The bed filled most of the room. The only light was on a small table next to the bed. The red shade was plastic and faded and it made the lamp give off a sort of pink haze. The whole scene was so sad and sleazy it made me want to puke.

I stood by the door, resting my fingers on the handle, not sure if I should even bother walking into this bloody nightmare. If I sound shocked then, fair enough, I'll put my hands up to that. You might think that a bloke like me, just let loose after a twelve stretch, would welcome a bit of professional attention, but all of this was new to me. I had never been involved in the porn business or got hooked up with pimps and tarts. I was a straightforward fighter. And I've never paid for a shag in my life.

The girl forced a smile up at me as I closed the door. She looked like she was on slapper-auto-pilot, if you know what I mean.

Her smile was meaningless.

"Hello," she said.

"You Jenny?" I asked.

"That's right, I'm Jenny. What's your name?"

"Tony."

"Come and sit beside me, Tony."

She patted the bed beside her hesitantly. Her words sounded like they were coming from a robot rather than a living, breathing human being.

I hesitated at first, then thought I'd better go and sit next to her. She couldn't have been a day over 15. She had the unformed body of an adolescent and her eyes lacked that sour, cynical look of older tarts.

Yet here she was trussed up to look like a time-served whore in a tight silk miniskirt with a slit up the side showing a hint of stocking tops, and a white see-through blouse with a black bra underneath.

Sitting less than a foot from her I could see she had bruises all over one side of her face. They'd been badly disguised by heavy make-up.

"Where you from, Jenny?" I asked, feeling more like a father then a punter.

"I'm from here," she said, her head nodded slightly. She was nervous.

Then she bent forward unexpectedly, thrusting her face down on my knees, pushing her head into my lap.

I felt her lips trying to work on me through the fabric of my trousers so I pulled her head away with my hand and turned my body towards her so she couldn't do it again.

"Leave it out," I said.

"What can I do to please you?" she slurred.

"I just wanna talk."

"Ssh!" She pointed to the door. "He's out there listening. He'll be angry if you don't come out happy."

"I'm happy," I said, but I didn't mean a word of it and she knew it.

"He thinks I'm no good. But I am good, aren't I?"

"You're good."

"You can talk now," she said, "but keep it down."

"Where d'you get the bruises, Jenny?"

"What?" she said. She looked even drowsier than earlier. "What did you call me?"

Her head was dropping to one side as she spoke.

"Jenny?" I looked straight at her as I spoke.

She didn't respond. But I could see fear watering up in her eyes.

"What's your real name, love?" I asked as gently as I could.

She looked at the ceiling. "Lorna."

"Let me see," I grabbed her right hand and looked at it in the light. Two crude hearts had been drawn on her hand with a blue ballpoint.

"Who did this?"

"He did ... he said it was what you wanted."

"Did he hit you?"

"He gets angry."

He was starting to make me pretty fucking angry, too. This wasn't the girl I was looking for. Even her accent wasn't from London. How she'd got herself into this mess was none of my business. That didn't stop me feeling sorry for her, but I couldn't fight the whole vice business on my own, even if I wanted to, I which definitely fucking well didn't.

I asked her: "Where you from, Lorna?"

"Macclesfield."

"That's a shame."

"What?"

"I'm lookin' for someone else ... the real Jenny."

Then she lowered her voice, trying to make it seductive. "Don't say that. Please don't say that."

"Will he hit you again?"

"Yes."

She tried to force herself back in my lap again and I had to push her away. Then, holding her head in both hands I said to her: "Now listen to me, Lorna. He's not goin' to hit you."

"Not if you're happy."

"I am happy. I told you."

She looked as if she was about to burst into tears.

"Please tell him that. Please tell him I made you happy."

"I will."

"Promise me, Tony. Promise me."

"I promise. But I gotta go now. Don't be frightened. All right?"

She nodded her head like any 14 or 15-year-old kid would. Just like my daughter would.

I stood up slowly, backing away. She sat there huddled in a ball, about to start sobbing, terrified she was going to another kicking for something she hadn't done. Something I had not let her do.

I kept thinking about what I'd do if this was my kid. I let myself out of the room and gently closed the door behind me.

I leaned against the wall in the corridor for a few moments, shaking my head, wondering how I could have been so stupid. There had to be an easier way than this to find Jenny.

As I started heading for the top of the stairs I realised someone was standing there in the shadows. He moved towards me.

"Happy?" he asked me.

I looked up as he swaggered towards me. He was full of it. If they had an award for Cunt of the Year he would come first, second and third.

"Yeah ... Yeah, I'm happy."

"She make you feel good?"

I shook my head again. I had to sound convincing. I took a deep breath.

"Yeah. She really knows what she's doin'."

"Seventy-five."

The man was a tall and muscular — a Turk or an Arab, dressed in a flash suit made out of shiny blue material. He seemed to fill the passageway, and stood at least three or four inches taller than me.

I took out a bundle of notes and began counting 75 into his hand. It was only then that I realised my hands were shaking. It took all of my self-control to stop me from smashing his sneering fucking face to a pulp. Teach him a lesson he'd never forget.

But I knew that would only result in that poor kid Lorna getting yet another pasting. As I stood there I was grinding my teeth so hard that I thought they'd start cracking.

"She a good girl, Jenny. One o' my best, my friend," he said, proudly.

"Very good. The tops," I muttered.

"You come back any time you want. She be here."

"I will, I promise."

"Just ask fa me."

"What's your name?"

"Abdullah. They call me Turkish Abdullah."

Turkish Abdullah walked me to the top of the stairs. He even put his arm around my shoulders in a really greasy way. I was disgusted and I gripped my fists hard to stop me using them on him. But he didn't follow me down the stairs.

As I reached the landing below I heard fast-moving footsteps on the bare boards above, followed by the sound of a door being opened.

Somewhere, someplace that poor kid's parents were worrying themselves sick about their little girl.

16

It took me a while to find a cab in Devons Road so I was cutting it a bit fine by the time I got back to that pub in Canning Town. I trotted into the lobby having worked up a bit of a lather, certain that Jimmy The Mole would be waiting there to give me a hard time.

I was in such a state I didn't even notice the same piece of muscle from earlier move alongside me as I walked in and then tap me on the shoulder.

"You got a moment?" he said.

"What's the problem?"

"You work for that toerag who's upstairs with my guv'nor, right?"

"What?" I said, still convinced I knew this bastard from somewhere in the past.

"He's not goin' to pay up no more."

"What you on about? I'm just havin' a quiet pint."

"Don't gimme that. I know what your game is."

"Fuck off."

"Don't say I didn't warn you."

With that he retreated, which surprised me. But I presumed he'd soon be back with a few friends.

Then The Mole came down the stairs at high speed, a grim expression on his face.

"On your bike, sunshine," he said to me. I took off after him as he marched towards the exit.

A few seconds later, we were about to get in the Merc when that muscle-bound Muppet stepped out of the shadows and prodded me on the shoulder again.

Then he ran a finger across his own throat menacingly.

"You two are for the chop."

He was so close to me I felt his spit hit my nose as he spoke.

I squeezed my right fist tight and gave him a powerbreaker. His teeth connected to my knuckles in a soft crunching sound.

Then his head hit the pavement a split second later.

"What the fuck d'you do that for?" spat out Jimmy The Mole.

"He was askin' for it."

As we got into the car, The Mole looked down at The Muppet still spark out on the ground and said quietly: "Hope you haven't fuckin' killed him."

I reversed out of our parking space narrowly missing the minder's right leg. Moments later I took a glance in my rear-view and saw him stumbling around holding his head.

"He'll live," I said.

As we pulled out of the car park I spotted the muscleman struggling to pull something out of his inside jacket pocket. I thought it would be a shooter. But it turned out to be a little notepad, and he was scribbling something in it ... a thank you note? Was it bollocks! He was taking down my number plate.

"He's on to us," I said as we drove off.

The Mole turned around and saw what I saw.

"That lot 'ave been on my back for weeks. Let's go. I'm runnin' late."

As was becoming traditional between me and The Mole, a long stretch of silence followed ...

At the end of the evening, as we drove back towards The Mole's place in Dalston, I decided it was time to have a chat about other things.

"I been askin' around about Jenny."

"And?"

"It's not goin' to be easy."

"No one said it would be. Get to the point."

He sounded a bit impatient. But I ignored it.

"While you were at that first boozer this evening I popped out to see someone. Met a girl of about fifteen on the game. She had bruises all over her face."

"What was her name?"

"It wasn't Jenny," I said. "The geezer who set it up claimed her name was Jenny but they were having me on. It wasn't your girl."

"You sure?"

"You don't sound like you're from Macclesfield."

"What?"

"Don't worry about it," I replied.

We reached The Mole's street, and I dropped him off without exchanging another word of conversation.

That young kid Lorna weighed heavily on my mind that night. I kept comparing her to my own daughter, Karen. Her predicament bothered the hell out of me, to be honest about it.

About four o'clock the next day I found myself sitting in the Merc in a Hoxton sidestreet watching the kids leave school. I hadn't planned to do it and I didn't have a clue what I wanted to happen, but there I was, desperately looking for Karen.

She got out late, walking along with two friends, arms linked, but she didn't look very happy. I stared at her through the windscreen, wondering how the hell I could sort out what had happened between her mother and me.

She was about to pass me, unnoticed, when she glanced sideways in my direction and our eyes met. She looked surprised, but instantly unlinked arms with her mates and stopped dead in the street. Her friends carried on a few paces, then stopped to wait for her.

She walked over to the passenger window, and I leaned across to unwind it.

"Is this your motor, dad?"

"Yeah. D'you like it?"

"It's wicked," she said with a real glint in her eyes.

"They don't make 'em like this any more."

"Can I get in?"

"'Course you can." I pushed open the door for her, and after a smile to her friends Karen climbed in beside me. The girls giggled, and went off down the road.

"Bet they're dead jealous," she said, with a hint of satisfaction.

"Good mates of yours?"

"Sort of."

She sat back in the old leather seat, stroking it with her hand, looking around the inside of the car admiringly. Then she sat forward to look at the radio/tape player. I pressed a knob on the dashboard and the aerial went up and down automatically.

"Want a ride home?" I asked, almost nervously.

"All right."

"I'll go the long way round then we can have a chat."

After another inspection of the inside of the car, Karen said: "You caused a lot of aggro the other day, dad."

"I know. I'm sorry."

"So you should be."

"What did your mum say afterwards?"

"Nothin'. She never talks about you."

"What? Never?"

She stared at me and then raised her eyebrows before rocking backwards and forwards nervously.

"Never."

Then Karen turned and looked out of the window as she spoke.

"Why d'you two split up?"

"Didn't she tell you?"

"Nope."

"Then I can't, either," I said.

"Come on. I've got a right to know."

"I got in a bundle of trouble, Karen."

"We all know that. You only just come out."

She was still looking out of the window as she spoke.

"But why did you really split up? Didn't you love her no more?"

"Love her?" I answered. "I never stopped lovin' her."

"Well then it's daft, 'cause I know she loves you."

"It just ain't that simple, sweetheart."

"Why isn't it?"

"I'll tell you about it some day."

I knew that was a bad answer. The wall of silence that followed simply confirmed it.

We got stuck in a traffic jam on the Mile End one-way system close to where Karen and her mum lived. I'd taken the long route, but the school was still only a short walk away.

Eventually I pulled over to the side of the road.

"Off you go, then," I said. "Your mum'll be worryin' about you."

"She's more worried about you."

Karen leaned over and pecked me on the cheek.

"Will you pick me up from school again?"

"Your mum wouldn't be too happy about that."

"I can keep a secret."

I grinned at her.

"Well, will you?" she asked.

"Maybe ... when I can. I'm workin' most days."

She was about to get out of the car when she stopped herself and turned back towards me.

"Can you do any tricks?" she said.

"What sorta tricks?"

"You know, tricks. Dads are meant to do that sort of thing with their kids."

"Well, I'm not sure ... D'you mean this kind of thing?"

I took a 10p coin from my pocket and made it pirouette along my fingers.

"Now you're a real dad."

She was smiling, but we both knew I'd have to pull off a lot more dificult tricks than that to really be her real dad again.

"Off you go, Karen."

"See you, then."

"Next time ... when I can."

I stared after her as she walked towards the estate. I felt sad. I felt jubilant. I felt lonely.

But I was glad she hadn't suffered like I did when I was a kid.

17

I doubt if the taxi driver knew what a fateful journey this was for his young passenger on that March morning in 1967. But he must have known something was up from the dreadful sadness that filled the air when he drew up outside Dr Barnardo's 'Ever-Open Door' at Stepney Causeway, E.1.

My stepdad grabbed me by the arm and dragged me into the building. I was terrified and began crying — I knew what lay in store for me. He held so tightly onto my wrist I thought he'd snap it in two, but I still fought like a fucking terrier.

I broke away from him and tried to run down the hallway, sobbing and shouting — my screams echo in my mind to this day and I still wake up shivering whenever that old, familiar nightmare kicks in.

I remember that on one side of the Dr Barnados hallway was a hatch a bit like the ticket office at a railway station. My stepdad stood there talking to someone on the other side of it. I couldn't hear what they were saying because I was making such a racket, but I noticed him signing some documents.

That was it, the final abandonment, signed away like a piece of lost property. Not even fucking lost — just unwanted. I don't remember what happened after that. I don't even recall a single incident for the following couple of weeks, although I know I was given the sort of tests and medical examinations.

On April 21 1967 I was transferred from that Barnardo's headquarters in Stepney to their home for 'backward' children up in Bedford, about 70 miles north of London.

It was a big, cold, scary-looking place called Cardington Hall. Huge rooms. High ceilings. Lots of pictures of Jesus and his apostles. The floor was so highly polished you'd notice a drop of sweat glistening on it. It was like being in another world — and I hated every bloody minute of it.

Up a great oak staircase was a long gallery where there were several vast rooms — the children's dormitories. These funny-looking kids ran out of the rooms as I walked in the hallway below and began peering down at me through the banisters. Then a bunch of older boys and girls appeared from the other end of the house. They must have been 14 or 15, I suppose.

The matron who was walking alongside me called

one of them over — a fat boy — to take care of me. That meant kitting me out with a school uniform — a pair of shorts, a blue turtle-neck jersey and a crappy jacket. Then he took me up the stairs to the piss-smelling dormitory where I would sleep. My life in hell had begun.

But even that smell wasn't as bad as the pong of a Nit Inspection. Once a month the matron would line us up and plough through our hair with a sharpened fine-toothed comb; this alone was painful because the teeth would dig into our scalps and make our heads sore and covered with more scabs than any bloody lice could inflict. At least, that's the way it seemed to me at the time.

But that was nothing compared to the shame that came if you were found to be carrying the dreaded lice. Then we had to rub this evil-smelling ointment into our scalps and wear a towel wrapped round our heads like a turban.

That provoked a lot of barnies with other kids who'd call us 'poofs' and stuff like that. That was a worse punishment than anything the people in charge could dole out.

Rules were made not to be broken and God had to be prayed to daily for forgiveness even when I hadn't done anything wrong.

There was nothing wrong with my head that a bit of patient care and understanding couldn't have cured but, as a kid, I didn't really give a monkey's about anything.

I'd run backwards outside the principal's office and

get a bollocking for my troubles, followed by some meaningless, time-consuming chores as punishment. The punishment was for being out of bounds, not running backwards, or so they told me. The worse they treated me, the more I rebelled. That soon got me classified as a hopeless case.

I wasn't much good at most classes except visual things like art and I did enjoy listening to English history. There was nothing I liked better than to sit back and lose myself in a distant imaginary world as the teacher read grisly tales of bloody murder in the Tower of London and corruption in high places.

After becoming a Barnardo's boy I decided not to tell anyone when my real birthday was. Eventually, I even started to doubt my real age.

Strangely enough, this had a few advantages because I used to celebrate my birthday whenever I felt like it, sometimes twice or even three times a year. I'd simply wake up one morning, and decide that today was my birthday and tell everyone to congratulate me and give me presents.

Every now and again I was shipped out of Cardington Hall to some foster family or other to see if I was fit to be let back into the real world. But I never hit it off with any of the adults. They all seemed to hate kids. It made me wonder why the hell they were so desperate to look after troublesome little gits like me.

Eventually, as I hit my teens, I was shoved into another Barnardo's place in Kingston-Upon-Thames, followed by a spell in one of their halls in Hertford. More try-outs at foster families followed. But each time I'd blow it and be sent back to Barnardo's. Over the years I've seen several TV programmes where Barnardo's has been held up as a brilliant organisation that's saved the bodies and souls of countless kids like me. Well, I'm sure that's the case, but I'm afraid I wasn't one of them.

Not surprisingly, I got booted out of the entire system when I was 15 and went to live with my Uncle Billy in Hoxton. He was about the only adult I ever got on with.

Uncle Billy gave me some space and in exchange I didn't cause him too much grief. Looking back on it, he didn't exactly give me much guidance. His missus and him were always at each other's throats and I tried to keep out of the house most of the time.

When I turned 18 my Uncle Billy gave me a load of documents on my fostering. He told me he thought I was old enough to know why I'd been locked away in foster homes.

This is what they wrote:

PRIVATE & CONFIDENTIAL

ANTHONY FRANCIS MILLS. (Illegitimate)
Admitted 24.3.67
BORN: 11.9.1956 at Bart's Hospital,
Whitechapel.
BAPTIZED: C. of E. No particulars.
Mother C. of E.

LAST SIX MONTHS ADDRESS: c/o Mr James Kenton, Flat 9b, Onslow House, Hoxton. N1 (Stepfather)
LAST SCHOOL ATTENDED:
St Ignatius Primary, Noble St, N1.

PAYMENT:	PERIOD:	AGREEMENT:	INFORMATION
See Below	*Six months*	*None.*	*FROM:*
	probation		*Report(Kim)*

APPLICANT: Mr James Kenton, SEE ABOVE.

MOTHER: Beatrice Jennifer Kenton née Mills (30); health good; character indifferent, separated from husband (see above); last known address — Flat 9b, Onslow House, Hoxton N1.
FATHER: (Putative): Frank Charles Booth (38); Van driver; £1,050 per annum; Durham Road, Eltham, SE12
MOTHER'S HUSBAND: See above; married the mother 12.12.61 at Bow Road Register Office; no other particulars.
HALF-BROTHER OR SISTER: Child of the mother's marriage, no other particulars.

The mother is described as an adventuress. At the time she met the putative father, she was a cleaner in a factory. She married in 1956, and her present address is unknown. When last heard of, two years ago, she was separated from her husband, and the child of that marriage was left to virtually fend for himself.
The putative father is the son of a convicted

burglar and living at a number of hostels. After Anthony was born, the putative father was due to pay the mother through a solicitor the sum of £500 in order to clear his name but he never did. Early in 1967 the mother's new husband was physically attacked by Anthony. Mr Buttle, of the Church of England adoption society, was asked by Mr Kenton to get Anthony adopted. For a short time he paid £5 a week while Anthony was in the society's home at Kingsbury. Anthony was sent to several people with a view to adoption, but each time he was returned with such excuses as being untruthful, dishonest and unintelligent.

Two years ago, he was boarded out by applicant with a Mrs A., at Prittlewell, Essex, for about four months prior to last September. He was then brought to London and handed over to the care of a Mr and Mrs M., of White Hart Lane, Tottenham, N.10, who contemplated adopting him. On 12.2.66 Mr M took him back to applicant, as not being suitable. Applicant stated he could not afford to keep Anthony so he had to go into another home.

Anthony is a weak-looking child and mentally backward, but he has never had a chance, being pushed about from pillar to post. At school he was said to be quite docile and friendly. The putative father should be persuaded to contribute regularly towards Anthony's maintenance.

F.M.A.

I discovered things about my background I didn't

even want to know about. The first page is what knocked me sideways the most.

Until then I didn't know it was my horrible stepdad who forced Barnardo's to take me. He kept telling me he didn't want me to go. I didn't even know I had a "putative father", as they call him, who was supposed to have helped support me.

Now you know why my daughter Karen's welfare was so especially important to me.

18

Anyway, back to grim reality and the present day — the next day, in fact.

This time I missed Karen but I was still too early to meet Jimmy The Mole, so I wasted time driving around in my car, waiting for the mobile to start singing so I could be on my way. First I floated over to High Holborn to see an old mate, then I headed east to Whitechapel.

I even went down the road under the bridge that ran past The Surprise Club. In daylight it was just dreary, dirty and deserted except for a few used condoms and beer bottles in the gutter. Commuters were heading towards the station, heads down against the drizzle, clutching newspapers, brief cases and shoulder bags.

Halfway along the road, I slammed my brakes on. That same girl, Lorna — the one who'd said her name was Jenny — was walking along the street.

She was wearing exactly the same outfit she'd been wearing the night I entered that little room; miniskirt, see-through top, black bra. But out in the open air she looked even younger and more pathetic.

My sudden braking alerted her to me and she squinted in my direction. Her eyes were glazed with dope.

I leaned across and wound down the passenger window.

"You're out early," I said.

She barely looked at me. She was so out of it she was resting her hand on the bonnet to stop herself falling over. Then she looked directly at me and her face changed expression instantly.

"What you doin' here? You told him, didn't you?"

At that moment I spotted that she had two fresh bruises on the right side of her face.

"Told him what?" I said, knowing full well what she was on about.

"You told him and he ..." she hesitated, "... just fuck off and leave me alone."

She turned and walked off down the street, wobbling on heels that were too high for her.

I slung the car in reverse and tried to get level with her before stopping again.

I shouted: "I didn't tell him nothin'!"

"Fuck off!"

She continued walking.

I leapt out of the car, ran after her and caught her.

"Fuck off!" she screamed at me again.

"I wanna know what he did to you!"

"You don't care. You're just sayin' that."

"I want to know."

She hesitated and looked straight at me.

"He took all my gear, and then he ..."

She started crying.

I got out of the car and put my forearms gently around her shoulders, not wanting to hug her properly in case she turned on me and started fighting me off.

"I know you told him," sobbed Lorna.

"I only told him what a great time I had."

"He knew ... you must have said somethin'."

My Merc was still sitting in the middle of the road with its engine running.

"Come on," I said. "Let's get a cup of tea."

"I don't drink tea."

"Coffee then!"

Her clouded eyes looked anxiously at me, like a pet dog trying to keep her master happy.

"Can I have a milk shake?"

"All right, let's get you a milk shake."

We found a caff just up the road. Lorna followed me in and we sat at a greasy table next to the window.

"So what d'you fancy then?" I asked. "Vanilla? Chocolate?"

"Butterscotch."

"Butterscotch? They might not have that."

"They'll have it."

"All right. Stay there."

I went to the counter, ordered the milk shake and a cup of tea for myself. Then I sat back opposite her.

"What d'you really want from me?" asked Lorna.

"Just to talk."

"You mean talk dirty?"

"I'm tryin' to find someone."

"Who?"

"A friend of a friend. A girl like you. She's called Jenny."

"My name's Lorna."

"Yeah ... but you said you was called Jenny."

"I'll say whatever you want me to say."

She looked away, across at the road under the bridge. It was starting to get dark.

"You sure you didn't tell him, mister?"

"Cross my heart," I said, miming the action.

"All right, I believe you ..." She looked past me, over my shoulder, towards the counter. "... there's my milk shake."

I got up from the table, and went to the counter. I didn't have enough change and the woman kicked up a right fuss about changing a tenner. By the time I turned round to return to the table, Lorna had gone.

I swore out loud, dumped everything on the table, and rushed out into the street. There was no sign of her. I looked both ways down the road, then crossed through the thick traffic and headed towards the area where I'd bumped into her.

I'd just reached the crossroads when a red beemer slowed for the corner, and then turned into the traffic.

Lorna was sitting in the back, staring vacantly out of the window. I tried to move towards her and raised my hands.

The driver looked across at me. I recognised him instantly. He was the bastard who was outside Lorna's door at the club, the one who called himself Turkish Abdullah.

That evening I was back with Jimmy The Mole, and facing yet another night of driving and waiting, driving and waiting.

The next afternoon, after a delivery of booze and fags, I went back to the Go Go club off Devons Road. The sign outside was not switched on and no one was at the door. As I walked in, I started thinking about that poor little kid Lorna and how those slimy bastards had tried to con me by getting her to say her name was Jenny.

As luck would have it, I bumped straight into Ian, the toerag who'd taken me up the stairs to meet Lorna. He was sweeping the floor of the clubroom with a half-smoked cigarette behind his ear.

He didn't look up at first, but I soon got his attention when I cracked my elbow down on the back of his neck so hard that he smashed a wooden chair topieces on his way to the floor.

"I've come about that young girl," I said, standing over him with one boot pressing down on his windpipe.

Ian looked up very nervously.

"What bird?"

I leaned down and whacked him straight across the face. I swear I felt his teeth wobble.

"Don't take the piss."

His eyes were swimming in yellow fear.

"Where's that little kid you had in the room up there?"

"She's not around," he mumbled, a blob of blood dribbling out of the corner of his mouth.

That just got me even more fucking annoyed.

"I said, where is she?" I barked at him through gritted teeth.

"I dunno. I swear I dunno. They come and go all the time."

I grabbed him by the front of his shirt, squeezed tight and started lifting him off the ground. All the old anger and fury kicked in at that moment.

Then I stopped and held him in mid-air. It dawned on me the only person who'd suffer if I bust his head open on the floor would be that poor kid, Lorna. So I put him down but still held him by the scruff of his neck.

"She must be somewhere."

Just then my mobile started singing. I didn't want to let go of this slimy bastard until I was sure he'd told me everything.

The phone kept ringing.

"Hadn't you better answer it?" he croaked, struggling to breathe. Maybe I was holding on to him a bit too tight.

As the phone kept on singing I squeezed his neck even tighter. His eyes looked like they were about to pop out of their sockets.

"Watch your back, sunshine," I grunted and let him go.

He nodded so hard I thought his head would snap off. I pulled out the phone, flicked it open and put it to my ear.

"Yeah?"

19

I was on my third delivery of booze and fags that day — thankfully only a small one — when I left the Merc on a double yellow line in Homerton High Street.

I got the boxes out of the back, slammed the boot lid and headed towards the shop where I was dropping off.

It was a new location — a crummy little newsagents, much smaller than most of the places I usually delivered to. Empty porno video boxes were neatly displayed on clean shelves alongside skin flicks and a modest selection of regular newspapers and magazines.

"Here you go," I said as I dumped the first of the cartons of fags.

The kid standing by the till jerked his head towards a narrow door at the back of the shop.

"In there, mate. Mick'll check 'em off."

I walked on through, having to turn sideways to get through the doorway with the big box in my hands.

Another man was sitting at a desk, with a pile of paperwork in front of him.

"You Mick?" I asked.

"Yeah. What you got?"

"Six boxes."

"Put 'em down there. I'll 'ave to count 'em."

I lowered the boxes to the floor, then stepped back as Mick ripped open the tape that sealed the first one, and began pulling out the fag cartons. I glanced around the tiny room.

These sort of places always had a room like this: the stuff out front was tame porn mags and videos, or most of it was, and it was there for your average punter.

When the Old Bill busted them, the tapes out front were the ones they took away, looked at, sometimes prosecuted over ... and never returned. They were usually nothing more than copies of copies with interchangeable titles and boxes.

Many of them were even faked up with magazine photos that had nothing to do with the contents. But then no one ever asked for their money back.

But the material in the backroom was a different kettle of fish. To start with, it wasn't there for the Filth because it was not on public display. The owners would cover their arses by claiming the back room contained material that had been wrongly delivered or was for the personal use of the proprietor.

In reality, the back room was for the specialist customers. The rich and deeply sick and twisted. You could only get in the back room if you'd been personally recommended by someone in the know, or if you flashed enough wedge at the kid on the front desk. The rules hadn't changed since the days when I'd occasionally run deliveries to earn a few extra bob between fights.

When I got to the so-called specialist stuff, some of it really turned my stomach. The obsessive, detailed attention to one sick perversion after another made me realise just how fucking weird some people could be. An 18 stone gorilla who wants to rip my head off I can deal with — he doesn't frighten me. I know where he's coming from. But how the fuck do you figure out what's going on inside the heads of these sick pervos? They frighten me.

As Mick carried on counting the fags I wandered along the shelves picking up a magazine or two and glancing at the odd tape.

Then one caught my attention: it had a small colour photo on the box, which was unusual in itself. But this one got my attention for another reason.

The picture showed a girl dressed in rubber underwear, holding a whip and a long metal chain, about to give some bloke who was chained to the wall with a dog collar round his neck (I kid you not) a bloody good thrashing. Daft bastard deserves everything he gets, was my first thought, but then I noticed something even more strange about the girl. She had a tattoo on her hand — a heart within a heart. It was Jimmy The Mole's daughter.

I took the tape down off the shelf and studied it more closely.

Behind me, Mick announced: "It's all here."

I turned round and held up the tape.

"Can I borrow this one?" I asked.

Mick shrugged and then winked at me. "No problem."

"How much?"

"Have it."

"You sure?"

"You're in the firm, ain't you?"

I grinned.

"See you around."

Just then my mobile started ringing. I answered it.

"Yeah. All right. Where?"

I put it down again.

"No peace for the wicked," said Mick, winking again as I headed for the door. Christ knows what sort of a wanker he must have thought I was.

On my way back to the car I stopped at a newsagent's and bought a big brown envelope. I slipped the video inside, then wrapped the paper tight around it and squeezed it into my coat pocket.

The address I'd been given on the phone turned out to be one of the more upmarket strip joints in Hoxton. The pictures outside had been tastefully airbrushed and all the photos were displayed in sturdy glass cabinets.

The foyer even had a fountain and a fish pond. The box office was more like a West End theatre, plush red carpet and heavy drapes everywhere.

I strode through the foyer without a sideways glance, and pushed open the first door that was marked PRIVATE.

Inside the office was that slimy git Kenny, who'd set me up with "Jenny" in the other clip joint. He swung round the moment I walked in and tried to get past me. I stopped him with a mighty right hander to the gut. He doubled up and then tried to wind me with a head charge to the stomach.

I smashed my fist down on his back hard as he tried to force me up against the wall. Then I grabbed a handful of his hair, yanked his head back and booted him in the bollocks with sickening crunch. He went down screaming and clutching his goolies.

"You're like a bad penny, you are ..." I said, sinking my right toecap into his kidneys. He squealed and for an instant his hands shot out from around his nuts. They went straight back in again, though. I couldn't tell whether he was fondling them or counting them. "... you pop up in all the wrong places."

I pulled him up onto his feet and he stood there, whimpering, still cupping his assets. He looked at me a bit sheepish then.

"You should stick to washin' spunk off the walls." I grabbed his chin between my thumb and forefinger and squeezed very hard. "What happened to that girl?"

"What girl?"

"The one you set me up with, the one you said was called Jenny."

"What about her?" he was mumbling now, mainly on account of the fact I was controlling the movement of his mouth.

"I hear she's gone awol," I said.

"So?"

"I wanna find her."

"So do lots of geezers."

"I said where is she?"

"Haven't a fuckin' clue, Tone. One minute they're here, next minute they're gone."

He gestured with his thumb, behind him.

"You'd better get upstairs. He's waiting for you."

I stepped past him, then paused.

"Kenny?" I said, letting go of his chin.

"Yeah."

"There's somethin' I'd like to know."

"What's that then?"

"How come he phoned me?"

Kenny shrugged his shoulders but said nothing.

Benny was sitting backstage. Someone had put a little round table out for him, with a white cloth and an ice bucket. He was sitting in a funny-looking plastic chair shaped like the palm of a hand.

A couple of strippers were on stage, rehearsing their dance routine. Benny was watching, pulling on a long, fat, smoky cigar. The girls were in their civvies. Their trainers made a clumping sound on the bare boards of the stage as they practised their steps.

Benny saw me approaching.

"Watcha, Tone."

"Hello, Benny."

"Sit yourself down somewhere ... how's the missus?"

"Don't see much of her these days."

"How about your kid?"

"She's alright."

Benny leaned forward and pulled a large green champagne bottle out of the ice bucket and swung it in my direction.

"It's my birthday today ... you know that? My fuckin' birthday."

"Happy birthday," I said, in a flat voice.

"Ain't you gonna ask how old I am?"

"How old are you Benny?"

"Fifty-nine, Tony. Fifty-fuckin'-nine. What about you?"

"It's not my birthday."

"Have a drink anyway."

There was a spare glass on the table, which Benny filled with bubbly. Then he passed it to me and topped up his own glass.

"Cigar?"

"No, thanks."

"You know what I think, Tone?"

"No. What d'you think, Benny?"

"I think you think I landed you in the shit."

"Well, you did, didn't you?"

"Life goes on, Tone, old son. We can't always control what happens. We can only swim around it."

"Yeah ... but what happens if you can't swim?"

"You drown."

Benny stared right at me in a strange kind of way as he said it. Then he took a long suck on his cigar and I knew that meant he was about to start lecturing me like he always did in the old days.

"You're always gettin' your knickers in a twist, Tone. And it's always over the little things. You know the little things ...?"

"What little things are those, Benny?"

Benny had always talked in bloody riddles. It really got on my wick.

"I mean," Benny said. "D'you or d'you not get confused?"

"Sometimes."

"At least you know it, Tone. That's half the battle."

"Suppose so."

"And that's important ... because you know what I'm good at?"

"No, Benny, I don't know what you're good at ..." I said, wearily.

"I'm good at those little things. Little things that mean everythin'. The things you forget. That's why I've still got the family. It's all on the level. And it's all thanks to the little things. And you're part of that family, Tone. One of my favourite members."

"What's your point, Benny?"

"My point is this ..." He paused and took a long look at me before grabbing that bottle of bubbly as if he'd just picked up a dead chicken by its neck.

"Here ... have some more champagne."

"No, thanks. Still haven't finished this."

"You seen round the place yet?"

Benny had clearly decided not to tell me what his point was.

"Only just got here."

"Then let me show you. You'll like it here ... it's got real class."

I followed Benny through the wings, and out onto the stage. The girls were still rehearsing, whirling and clumping in rhythm in their wedgy trainers. Benny pointed out all the special stuff he was proud of like the trapdoors, smoke machines, laser system and strobe lights. I nodded and nodded as he droned on and on. I tried to look interested but really I didn't give a fuck.

Then we headed back to Benny's table.

That was when I said: "So what's really on your mind, Benny?"

He took another long suck on his fat cigar while he contemplated his reply.

"Your happiness, that's what's on my mind. You served your time, you came out. I wasn't here, now I am here. I want you to know that I care about your welfare."

"Thanks," I said.

"So now you're busy, you got a job. Any complaints?"

"No."

"That geezer you're drivin' round. Is he up to anythin' I should know about?"

"What d'you mean?"

"I mean, is he diddlin' me?"

"Thought he was in the family?" I said.

"He is."

"Then you must know what he's up to."

"Tone, please, just keep an eye on him and let me know if he's up to any mischief."

"Why me?" I said.

"Because you drive him around. You should be keepin' an eye on these sorta things, little things. It might be a different business from the fight game, Tone, but the rules are just the same."

"So I noticed."

He paused.

"All I'm askin' is that you watch what he's up to and then you tell me. And I'll be happy. All right, my old son?"

Benny rose from his silly chair and dropped his fat cigar in the ashtray. I got up at the same time. Benny put an arm around my shoulder and began leading me to the exit.

"You didn't like me back in the old days, did you?" Benny said. "I worked you hard. Your fights were my bread and butter."

I looked at him sharply but didn't respond.

"Don't worry ... everybody hates me once in a while. But all that's changin'. I just want you to be happy, Tone."

"That's funny, Benny," I said. "Everybody I meet makes me happy these days."

20

As I recall, we were halfway through a long evening and a couple of appointments behind schedule with three or four more to go when The Mole barked at me: "Loughton, me old mate."

Seemed like a perfect opportunity to bring the subject up so I steamed in yet again.

"So what really happens over there?"

"What?"

"You and your mate, Julio Inglesias," I said.

"Mind your own fuckin' business."

"Only askin'."

"Well don't."

"Can't blame me, can you?"

"'Course I fuckin' can," he said.

He must have given my question some thought,

though, because, after a short silence, he chipped in:

"What d'you think happens there?"

"Well, that geezer's not part of your regular milk round."

"Yeah?" came The Mole trying not to sound like I'd hit it right on the nail.

"It's gotta be somethin' big?"

"Could be."

Then I had an idea.

"Is he somethin' to do with your kid?"

The Mole stared ahead at the road as we drove.

"He's just a mate I have a game of pool with him," he said, ignoring my last remark.

I snorted and clapped my hands against the steering wheel.

"Don't take the piss."

"I'm not," he paused. "That's what we do. Have a game of pool."

"You tellin' me you slide up to knobsville two, three times a week to have a game of pool? Pull the other one, it's got sawn-offs on it."

He smiled faintly and raised his eyebrows. Then his face changed expression and he turned towards me.

"Why you so fuckin' interested anyway?"

I could have told him a porky then, but there didn't seem much point.

"I been told to keep an eye on you."

"Who by?"

"Who d'you think?"

He didn't bother asking.

We'd just reached the familiar house with the

gravel driveway and a few seconds later I pulled the old Merc to a halt in its usual spot.

As Jimmy The Mole got out he said: "Make sure you tell your mate Benny about that game of pool."

Still holding the door open, he looked back at me. "Thirty minutes."

Then he walked confidently across the gravel and was met at the door by the usual white-coated servant. The door slammed shut behind them.

I settled down to wait but I was well narked. I'd marked The Mole's card and told him Benny was keeping tabs on him, but still he wouldn't cough what this was all about.

About five minutes later the servant turned up with a silver tray balanced on the fingers of one hand.

"I was asked to bring this to you," he said.

He lowered the tray, and I noticed that it held two Polaroid snapshots. I picked them up from the tray, and flicked on the overhead interior light as the servant scurried off.

I looked down at the photos; Jimmy The Mole and his rich mate, the Julio Ingelsias lookalike, were standing together at the end of a pool table almost as big as a tennis court. The room was decorated like a palace.

The Mole was wearing his dark blue suit and the Arab was in an immaculate three-piece job. They looked as if they were on reasonable terms in one photograph. In the other the Arab were staring straight at the camera while The Mole got ready to pot a ball.

In both photos there was a huge painting of some Arab geezer in full headgear above a fireplace behind them. It didn't mean a fucking thing to me.

I propped the photos up on the dashboard and left them there. But Jimmy The Mole never mentioned a word about them when he finally came out of the house and we got back to work.

At the end of the evening I finally plucked up the courage: "So what's Benny really up to?"

This time The Mole seemed happy to talk.

"He wants to rule the fuckin' world."

"Don't we all?"

"Yeah, but he's serious," said The Mole. "He's got himself in with a bunch of new mates who'll give him some real pullin' power."

"How's he done that then?"

"Through dozens of protection rackets like the one I front for him," said The Mole, as I slung the Merc up outside his block of flats

He continued: "Its even more effective if you back it up with a bit of high class blackmail."

He paused to open the car door.

"Good night, Tone."

Just before The Mole shut the car door I leaned across to him and grabbed his arm.

"I nearly forgot. Got somethin' important to show you."

"What?" he said impatiently.

"Can I come in for a tick?"

"Make it quick. I'm knackered."

Once inside the flat, I asked The Mole for a cup of tea.

He didn't like that on account of the fact he obviously wanted some shuteye, but he agreed and went into the kitchen.

While he was out the way I took the video tape from my pocket, crumpled up and threw away the envelope it was wrapped in, and flicked on his VHS and telly. Then I slotted the tape in.

"What you got to show me that's so bloody important?" The Mole called from the kitchen.

"It's a surprise."

"Don't like suprises," he said as he walked in with a couple of mugs and put them down on a coffee table.

I flicked the play button on the remote. Only problem was I hadn't checked to see if it had been rewound and it came on in the middle of the action, if you can call it that.

There was this painfully thin young blonde girl with a tattoo on her hand. She was wearing skin-tight rubber underwear and black rubber stockings with stilettos. She was so thin I could have circled her waist between my thumbs and forefingers. She was almost losing her balance on spiky, black leather six-inch heels.

She was in a clinch with a big dark-haired guy, although the camera was at such an angle you could only see his hairy stomach and crumpled, bulging jeans. The girl was caressing that bulge, then she unzipped him and went down on him. I can tell you here and now it wasn't pleasant.

I looked across at The Mole. He was gripping the arms of the chair with his hands and rocking back and forth. I didn't need to ask him if it was his kid.

Then the camera briefly cut away to the man's face. It was that fucker I'd met at the club who called himself Turkish Abdullah.

He and the young girl were looking at the screen like zombies. They were obviously both completely off their faces.

Then the girl screamed at the camera: "Turn it off."

The Mole pushed himself across me, grabbed the remote and flicked it off.

"Fuckin' hell! Fuckin' hell! Fuckin' hell! Fuckin' hell!"

He was shaking violently as he said it over and over again. It was only then that I noticed he was sweating like a pig.

"Fuckin' hell. Fuckin' hell."

We both sat there in complete silence for at least half a minute.

"Where d'you get this shit from?" he asked.

"At one of my booze an' fags drops. They had it on their rack."

"It's her ..." He was shaking his head from side to side. "I just can't believe it."

"Who's that geezer?" I asked.

"How would I bloody know?" he said, still shaking from side to side. "That's my girl on there. My baby girl."

"You sure you don't know who he is?"

Jimmy The Mole shook his head as he looked at me.

"I've seen him around the clubs," I told him. "He calls himself Turkish Abdullah."

The Mole paused and looked up at me.

"His real name's Anif."

"You do know him?" I shot up angrily. "What the fuck's goin' on?"

"I told you," The Mole muttered under his breath. "I tried to get her back before, but I failed."

"But if you knew who he was why didn't you go after him?"

"They kept goin' off together and I knew if he heard I was after them again he'd hurt her ..."

Then The Mole gave me another of those awkward looks. Like a kid who's about to spill the beans.

"You've been away a long time so I thought that'd give you a better chance of finding her."

"But you knew who this bastard was and you didn't tell me?" I said angrily.

"So what? You can handle yourself. You're The fuckin' Boss, remember?"

"That's not the point," I snapped back. "And you know it."

"Look, Tone, I'm a gambler," The Mole said to me. "I took a punt. Reckoned the odds were decent that you might track her down."

But I was still well pissed off about what was coming out of his stupid, ugly mouth.

"You set me up. I could have been fuckin' killed."

"Nah. The Boss is fuckin' invincible."

That last remark really wound me up. I caught him

full across the face. Not one of my specials, mind, but hard enough to let him know how I felt.

He gasped, and staggered back. Then he straightened himself out and looked right into me with his black, pinhead eyes. If he'd been packing a piece at that moment he'd probably have pulled it out and squeezed the trigger.

Instead, he pulled me right back down to earth.

"Shame I didn't fuckin' set you up."

He rubbed his stinging chin as he spoke.

"This ain't the ring and you ain't The Boss no more. Welcome to the real fuckin' world. You can't hurt me. I don't feel pain like you or any of those poor bastards you hammered in the ring. All I want to do is find my kid ...

"... that nutter Anif nearly killed me when I tracked 'em down last time. I just thought you'd stand a better chance than me. Anif controls my child, my flesh and blood, 24 hours a day. He's got her so pumped full of poison he's twisted her mind against me. And he lives off sellin' her body to any sick bastard who comes along."

The Mole looked close to tears as he spoke. After a few moments he paused to wipe his left eye with his finger and I reckon he was waiting for a response from me. The truth is, I didn't know what to say.

So he carried on:

"Anyone can have her. Any sadistic bastard who likes young girls. They'll kill her in the end," he said, his voice breaking up with emotion, "or she'll do herself in."

An image of my own kid came into my mind as he spoke. I knew I still had to find Jenny for him.

After he'd finished talking we stood there in complete silence.

At last I said: "Here ... drink your tea."

I passed him the cup but as soon as he took it off me he flung it straight at the TV set. It hit the screen full-on: the cup broke, but the screen didn't. Brown tea trickled down on to the carpet.

Then he looked across at me, and snorted out a mountain of breath.

I picked up the other cup and gave it to him. "Here, try this one instead."

21

It had been a week since I'd been able to get away early enough in the afternoon to see Karen, but I finally made it back to her school in Hoxton.

To be certain she didn't miss me I stood outside by the Merc, leaning against the gleaming silver front wing with my arms folded.

It was a bright, blue, clear day. My head was swimming with Jimmy The Mole, Benny and the search for Jenny. I had an ear-splitter of a headache. Felt like someone was sawing my brain in half.

Karen was the only real motivation I had at that moment. She made the future worth fighting for. She also made me hope and dream that one day I might get back with Brenda. Problem was, Brenda also happened to be the least accessible person of the lot.

I still loved Brenda. All I wanted was for things to get back to the way they were before. Hearing about The Mole's kid made me even more determined to try and get us together as a family again.

But I knew it wouldn't happen while I was ducking and diving for The Mole. As we went from pub to pub, mansion to mansion, picking up protection money, I sat in my motor or a tatty saloon bar churning it all over in my mind. None of it made much sense.

What the bloody hell was I playing at with Anif, Benny, Del and all the other stinking lumps of dog shit shifting along behind me? Soon they'd all be after me and I'd be trapped in Benny's family-from-hell forever.

I might survive keeping one step in front of them all, constantly on my toes, constantly keeping an eye out. But what sort of life was that?

That left Karen — the only rock of normality in this sea of shitty chaos.

So when she appeared amongst a crowd of her school friends I looked up and smiled happily. I was so relieved to see her. She immediately came over to me.

"Where you been, Dad?" she said.

I felt guilty before she'd finished saying it.

"Busy ... sorry." And I really meant it. "Told you I might not make it every day." We both climbed in the Merc.

"I know. But ..."

"Look at them," I said, interrupting her because I didn't want her to make me feel any more guilty. "Are they still jealous of you?"

"Hope so."

We moved off in the car and I slowly drove around in the hope of finding an even longer route back to her home.

"Did you tell her?"

"Mum? No ... but she guessed."

"How?"

"She always knows."

"Yeah. Mums always do. Specially yours."

Karen was staring into her lap, playing with the strap of her school backpack.

"I tried to talk to her about you," she said quietly.

"Don't bother."

"That's what she said, too."

I glanced across at Karen. She was looking right at me, waiting for a reaction. I felt yet more guilt cut right through me.

"What's wrong, Dad?" she said.

"What d'you think?"

"One day we might all get back together." She grinned at me. "That'd be really cool."

"Yeah, but I'm gettin' old, and I didn't treat your mum right."

"Tell me how you didn't treat her right?"

"Forgot she was there, y'know? Stupid, that, innit?"

"And I forgot you were there, until the other day. Stupid, that, innit?"

An hour or so after I'd dropped Karen off, a miracle occurred: Benny belled me on the Nokia. A second time.

We met in the same place, but the dancing girls

were nowhere to be seen.

Benny was in a nasty, edgy mood. I knew it from the moment I walked in. Bit like he'd been in the old days and, you know, the funny thing is that it made me feel better to see him this way.

I didn't like the new Benny pretending to be my friend because I knew there'd be a catch. He always wanted something from me and that afternoon I'd kept him waiting.

Benny was sitting in a cramped booth in the corner of the club when I strolled in. The stage was lit by a single spotlight that illuminated nothing but clouds of dust. Bit like a TV with the sound turned down.

"I need to know a few little things, Tone," he said out of the shadows.

"Like what?"

"Like what the fuck that toerag you're drivin' around is up to."

"There's nothin' to tell, Benny."

"What d'you mean, nothin'?"

"I mean nothin'. The opposite of somethin'."

"What about that Arab in Loughton who he sees? What's happenin' there?"

"Not much far as I can tell."

"Bollocks. I know he's tryin' to cut me out of that one."

"Cut you out, Benny? I don't know what you're on about. All I know is they have a game of pool together."

Benny let out a short, throaty laugh.

"Is that what he told you?"

"Yeah."

He looked at me kind of strangely then.

"Heard you kept your knuckles well oiled in the slammer."

"I had a reputation, if that's what you mean."

"Bet some of those psycho lifers had a right dig at you? They don't give a toss do they?"

"No worse than the rest of them."

"D'you take any big hits up here?" he asked, pointing at his own forehead.

"No more than the next man."

"You sure?"

"Get to the fuckin' point, Benny."

"I think you've lost it, old son."

"You reckon?" I said, not giving a flying fuck what he said. But he ignored my response.

"Now you listen to me, Tone. And listen real close 'cos I ain't gonna say this again! You're gonna find out exactly what that rodent is up to. Climb a drainpipe. Hide in a wardrobe. Take a photo ... just find out what's he's up to."

I sat there rocking back and forth on my chair looking him right in the eyes.

Then I said, very matter-of-factly: "Oh, I've already got a photo for you."

He stopped and looked straight at it as I handed it over. He waited a few seconds for me to say I was taking the piss. But I didn't.

Then I took the other Polaroid out of my pocket and also handed it to Benny.

A few feet away a stripper walked silently onto the stage wearing a tight shiny silver lycra bodysuit. She paced the stage in her platforms for a couple of moments and then started dancing even though there was no music on.

Every time her body twisted and gyrated it stretched the material into a second skin that followed every contour of her body. Then she began unzipping her costume at the front.

Benny didn't even give her a second glance. He couldn't take his eyes off those photos. Then his eyes snapped in my direction.

"You takin' the piss, Tone?"

I looked at him in such a way he knew I wasn't.

"I told you, Benny. All your man does is go in that flash house and play fuckin' pool. Why you got such a problem with that?"

Benny shot up from his seat so fast I thought he was about to pop one on me. I faced him off on the spot and got ready to drop him the way I should have done when he landed me in the shit years ago.

But Benny smiled and he was about six inches from my face.

"You're a right fuckin' comedian, Tone. You know that?"

I shrugged my shoulders.

"You should be doin' stand-up. Maybe I could become your manager. Bit like the old days, eh?"

"Ha fuckin' Ha," I replied.

On stage the girl had completely unzipped the front of her bodysuit to below her navel, exposing neat, pert breasts both pierced with tiny gold bolts. Very fucking classy.

She pushed one of her hands down inside the outfit so that you could see the back of her knuckles pressing against the skin-tight material. With her other hand she began stroking the bolt drilled through her left nipple.

Benny gave a brief glance then turned back to me.

"Bet they hurt when she had those bolts pierced through 'em. Makes your stomach turn, thinking about all that pain."

"What's your point, Benny?"

"Young Tracey up there," he nodded towards the dancer. "She told me the pain was worth it 'cos she liked the look of those bolts. Said it turned her on. You know what turns me on, Tone?"

He didn't bother waiting for a reply.

"What turns me on is power. And, sometimes, to get that power you have to do some dirty things. I mean nasty, kinky, slimy, filthy, sick and twisted. Anythin' you like — but not playin' a fuckin' game of pool."

Just then my old mate Del appeared quietly in the shadows, a couple of feet away.

Benny turned, and so did I. A second man was also standing in the half-light close to the stage, staring at the stripper as her routine got hotter and hotter. She'd pulled the entire top half of the bodysuit off so it hung down around her hips.

Then her hips started jigging around so fast it was like she was sitting on my Brenda's old spin drier. Suddenly the entire outfit was down round her ankles and she kicked it clear off the stage. Then she just stopped, gathered up her gear and walked to the front of the stage. There, under the full glare of that single spotlight, totally naked, Tracey called out: "Was that alright, Benny?"

Benny was looking straight at the man in the shadows. He said, without so much as even moving his eyes: "Perfect, darlin'. Perfect."

He got up and moved away from me and started weaving his way through the seats. Then he paused before turning back and looking towards me.

"Just find out what's happenin' ..." he gave me a watery smile, "... my old mate." And winked at me.

I could feel the tension tying knots in my stomach. I shut my eyes for a second, squeezed them tight and took a deep breath in the hope my anger would be gone by the time I opened them again.

Meanwhile, Benny linked up with the second man and they moved into the lighter area of the room. That was when I realised it was that Turkish bastard, Abdullah, or Anif or whatever his bloody name was.

My stomach started churning up again. Benny greeted him like a long-lost brother, hugging and slapping him on the back. Then Abdullah stared past Benny into the club, directly at me. His eyes were cold as steel and he had a nasty smirk on his face.

22

I'd decided not to confront Jimmy The Mole straight away about certain things because all the pieces of the jigsaw didn't yet seem to fit. In fact, I still didn't have a bloody clue what was really going on. I wanted to be certain of my facts before I steamed in.

That evening Jimmy The Mole emerged from a room behind the saloon bar of his first call of the day and we moved off towards the main exit at a furious pace.

He said quietly: "Get a move on. We're runnin' late."

"I been thinking ..." I said.

"That's not always a good idea."

"This is important."

"What?"

"Does he pack anything, this Anif geezer?"

"Yup."

"What? A shooter?"

"Yup."

"Does he ever use it?"

"Haven't a fuckin' clue."

We trotted out into the car park.

The Mole then said: "Why you askin' me all this?"

This time it was my turn to ignore his question. I knew he knew.

"Where to now?" I asked.

"The Fusilier." We were out in the street. He then glanced behind and hissed: "And fuckin' get your skates on."

I didn't sleep much that night. Carl was out when I got back and I spent at least an hour prowling back and forth across his living room floor trying to work out what my next move should be.

When Carl finally showed up I made out I'd only just got back myself. My brain was heavily overloaded with all the events of the past few days. I told Carl I was staying up for a while when he said he was off to bed.

Eventually I pulled out that bloody video tape again and slotted it into Carl's machine. This time I ran it from the beginning but kept the volume turned down, watching the flickering images in silence.

It made me feel even more uncomfortable than before. I kept trying to turn away from the really nasty stuff, but I couldn't stop watching it. I'd planned to fast-forward certain sections, but I never actually did.

The whole thing lasted about twenty-five minutes. When it finished I wound it back to the part with Abdullah in it. I froze the frame on his face.

Just then Carl appeared.

"Yo' need de real ting, my friend," he said. "Not dis shit."

I barely had the strength to look up at him.

"How long you been there?" I said.

"Long enough."

Carl plonked himself down in the other armchair.

"You see it all, then?" I asked him.

"Most of it." Carl looked across at me then. "Wot's up, my friend? Why yo' watchin' dogshit like dis?"

"Lots of reasons," I said.

Then we had a bevvy together and I told him the full story.

The next day I did my booze and fags rounds as fast as I could and by 3.30pm I was all done. I wanted to get to Hoxton and see my kid. But when the time came I headed off towards Benny's lousy club instead.

I hung about outside for a bit. It was located in the middle of a busy daytime street market so it wasn't too difficult to blend in with the crowds. After about half an hour my patience was rewarded when Anif came out of the club and strolled off down the street like a man without a care in the world.

Naturally I followed him.

He got to his red BMW, which was parked illegally

on a meter with a yellow cover over it. As he fiddled with the door and opened it I managed to get back to where I'd parked my car.

The congested one-way streets worked to my advantage because I managed to second guess where Anif would be sitting in traffic. I kept him in sight but made sure there were at least two cars between us.

It wasn't easy but I'd done it a few times in the past.

The name of the game is not to let them out of your sight, but to stay out of their sight as much as possible. There aren't many ways to do this. You can drive the rear left of the bloke you're trailing. That way he won't see you the whole time in his rear-view. But the number one rule is never spend too long trailing someone because in the end he's gonna spot you.

I followed him all the way to the Tottenham High Road. When Anif parked up on a spare meter I pulled over to the side of the street to see where he was going.

Anif moved across the pavement without even glancing in my direction and headed towards the green-and-red-painted door of a familiar blacked-out shop front, and entered. I was in luck. It happened to be probably one of the best-known basements in East London. It belonged to an old face called Barry Marshall who'd had the foresight to soundproof the walls when he came across all the soundproofing gear in a recording studio in Epping that was about to be knocked down to make way for a supermarket. I moved off to find somewhere to park my lovely old Merc.

Marshall let faces use his basement for a small

remuneration so they could test out their shooters. He even laid on grub and booze and a few ladies when required.

I waited outside the club for about an hour and then watched Anif leaving with a big grin on his face. Alongside him was Benny. They said their goodbyes and went their separate ways.

Now I knew for certain they were in some kind of partnership and that made me feel even more twitchy about what I was getting myself into.

Five minutes later I was shadowing Anif across London once again.

It didn't take long before he pulled into a small sidestreet in Finsbury Park. It happened so quickly I thought he'd sussed me out. But as I passed the end of the street I realised that Abdullah had simply spotted a spare parking spot.

I slung the Merc on a yellow line and scurried back to see what he was up to. I just caught him walking down an alleyway into another side street.

The buildings were really tightly packed and for a second I thought I'd lost him. I walked along the road trying to work out where the hell he'd gone. There were no obvious houses he could have dived into.

Then I noticed a church in the far corner just a short distance from where I'd last seen Abdullah. Without giving it much thought I walked across the road and went through the open double doors.

I slowed the moment I got inside. It felt cold and empty. Maybe all churches feel that way. How the fuck would I know?

Then I spotted someone in a pew towards the front of the church. As I moved forward I could see it was a teenage girl. She was sitting upright. Her head was raised and she was puffing at a fag.

I sat in the row right behind her.

I whispered: "You shouldn't be smokin' in a place like this."

She didn't respond but carried on staring straight ahead. She raised her cigarette for another puff, and as she did I saw the back of her right hand. She had a tattoo: two hearts bound together and pricked in blue.

"Jenny ...?"

She turned round and stared right at me. Her eyes had a glassy, vacant look.

"Your name Jenny?"

She didn't say a thing. Smoke drifted slowly out of her nostrils in thin streaks. Her face was deathly pale. Her eyes seemed to be watering.

"Put it out," I said, in the nicest voice I could manage under the circumstances.

She didn't respond but got up from her seat and walked unsteadily towards a cluster of candles on a sideboard. Then she carelessly stubbed the fag out in the soft wax on top of one of them.

She moved further away from me, edging down a narrow aisle on the side of the pews. She glanced towards me with a very scared expression on her face. She didn't have a clue who I was, of course, and I'd have been just as edgy if I'd been her.

She was scared, right enough, but her eyes remained as empty as polo mints. There was none of that bright awareness you see in the eyes of someone who knows he's in deep shit and, believe me, I've been nose to nose with enough blokes who were shitting themselves to know what I'm talking about. Jenny was zonked on something or other — heroin, crack, whatever.

I didn't want to freak her out, so I walked the other way down the centre aisle of the church, hoping to intercept her before she got out the door. But there was a raised pulpit in the way and I had to take a detour round it.

She never turned round but I could tell from the way she upped her pace that she knew she'd get out before me.

By the time I got outside the door she'd already disappeared from in front of the church.

I ran down the pathway. It was then I noticed Anif on the street corner with Jenny. He was walking her down the street towards the alleyway that led to his car. One of his hands was resting menacingly on the back of her neck.

She walked with him to his Beemer, climbed into the front passenger seat, and sat in silence as Anif fired up the engine.

They drove off, passing close by me. I shrank into a doorway. Jenny was staring straight ahead, into some remote, private world. I'm certain neither of them noticed me.

23

Jimmy The Mole's fears about security on his milk round prompted us to devise a safety system in case he ever had any real aggro during collections from boozers.

"If my number comes up on your mobile with a blank text message when I'm in with a punter then get alongside me pronto," he told me.

We'd both been concerned about that Muppet at the boozer in Canning Town. The Mole knew there would be more problems with him.

"Or we could get him on the pay role but I don't see why he should be allowed to take those sorts of fuckin' liberties."

I agreed.

So when it was time to go back to the same pub in

Canning Town we agreed to be extra vigilant.

As it turned out, I was running late. The Mole belled me on the mobile but I didn't hear it. He left a message saying he'd arrived and as there was no sign of the Muppet he was going up to see the guv'nor and I should wait in the bar when I got there.

The same barman was on duty as usual when I arrived. He even gave me a friendly nod that I didn't much like the look of.

Just then my Nokia started beeping to tell me I had a text message. The Mole's number came up on the screen. I walked past the barman and moved straight to the staircase behind the bar.

As I climbed the steps three by three to the first floor, cheesy muzac wafted out of speakers on the wall.

The first floor was deserted as always. I headed straight for the manager's office and knocked hard.

A long silence followed. Then I tried again. Even harder this time.

Then, from behind the door, a male voice said: "What d'you want?"

I didn't respond but knocked again with both fists which shook the door on its hinges.

"Open up!"

Another hard knock brought no response so I smashed my boot hard just below the main door lock.

Another beat of silence was followed by a rattling noise. The door opened only a few inches because it was secured by a chain. The lined face of an old geezer peered through the gap.

"What d'you ...?"

The moment he spotted me he ducked back out of sight and tried to slam the door.

I threw my whole body against it and heard it crack and then split around the chain bracket. I gave it an almighty shoulder charge as he tried to lock it.

The door splintered and swung open. I fell through the doorway and sent the old boy flying to the floor in the process.

The Muppet with the wide neck and cropped hair who'd tried to lean on us during the last visit stood there smirking at me. I still reckoned I knew him from somewhere. But I didn't wait for an introducion.

The sound of my fists pounding into his face was all the fucking "Hello" he was going to get out of me. I gave him a massive right hander and then jabbed at him with my left. Then another jab and another. It was all so fast he must have thought he was being attacked by a gang. He wobbled like a jellyfish then managed to recover his balance.

The twat took a massive swing at me and completely missed. When I saw his face snarling at me I knew where I'd seen him before. He'd been one of my lippiest challengers in Parkhurst. Couldn't put a name to his face, so I stuck my nut in it instead. I timed the headbutt to perfection and caught him right on the bridge of the nose. Now I remembered giving him a right thrashing back in the nick. This was turning into an action replay, but there weren't no slow motion involved. I was so fucking quick I was frightening myself.

I popped a healthy right into his gut. I felt his body jump on its legs. Then I started pounding away at him: left, left and then right — WHACK! Left, left and then right — WHACK! Air wheezed out of him with every shot. He couldn't cope with my speed. Every time I heard him catch his breath it spurred me on to give him another couple of belts.

It was all over in seconds. He was a crumpled heap on the floor dribbling claret all over the carpet. Sparko. Out like a light.

There I was worrying about middle age — The Boss was as sharp as ever. I might not carry quite as much young muscle as I once did, but I could still be a full-on fucking nut case when it mattered.

I rubbed the palms of my hands together to show that I considered I'd just done a good job and turned towards the old git. He'd been quivering in the corner of the room throughout my performance.

It was only then I realised he was at least seventy, grey and wrinkled. He scowled at me and then tried to get to his feet. Silly old bugger.

I pushed him back on the floor but he clung onto my leg, ripping at the fabric of my trousers. Now that made me very angry.

Then the old boy started howling so loud then that I had no choice but to whack him just hard enough to shut him up. I didn't want to cause him any real harm. But his glasses went flying.

Then I barged through the door to the main office where I found Jimmy The Mole slumped on a chair.

He'd been gagged and blindfolded and his head

was pulled back at an odd angle. His arms were stretched around behind his back and roped to the chair. His ankles had been tied to the chair, too.

I got to him and whipped off the blindfold. His eyes popped wide open with surprise.

"What's happened?" I said. The Mole arched his back, fighting against the restraints.

Behind me, some other bastard was coming straight at me.

Before he could get me I awarded him one of my finest brickhouse right handers and he crumpled to the floor like a demolition job on a sixties tower block.

Just then the old boy came scrambling into the room. I pushed him down to the floor. He stayed down on all fours and began groping on the floor for his glasses. I moved back towards The Mole, then felt something crunching under my foot and realised I'd just stepped on the old boy's glasses.

"Oh dear" I said.

I bent down, picked the specs up and held them to the light: One lense was cracked. I passed them to the old boy.

"Get in there," I yelled, pointing to a walk-in cupboard in the corner of the office.

He backed into the cupboard so fast he almost fell over a chair in the process. I slammed the door shut and shoved a chair up against it.

Then I bent over The Mole, and ripped the gag off him.

The old boy was starting to make a racket from the cupboard.

I ripped open the cupboard door, stooped over him, twisted his arm behind his back. I then dragged him on his knees out of the cupboard, gave him another right hander, then pulled open the door and threw him back in. He landed with a sickening crunch on the floor.

I slammed it shut and carefully angled the chair against the handle.

Then I returned to The Mole and completed undoing all his shackles.

"I found her," I said, breathlessly, as I ripped off the ropes.

"Where? Where is she?"

"She's on the manor."

The Mole and I were heading for the door when we both spotted a large bundle of £20 notes sitting on a desk and wrapped with a fat brown elastic band.

The Mole grabbed the cash and stuffed it in his briefcase.

"Hang about, that's not ours," I pointed out.

"Yes, it is," he said.

We were so diverted by the dosh that neither of us noticed the Muppet man stirring in the corner.

"You've had it," he mumbled at us.

I was going to give him some more treatment when The Mole pulled me back.

"What did you just say?" The Mole sneered at Muppet man.

"We'll 'ave you next time," The Muppet coughed back.

The Mole then opened his briefcase, dipped a hand

into it and pulled out a matt grey 9mm Glock semi-automatic.

My heart lost about three beats in a second.

"Want some of this?" he said, pushing the barrel right up this geezer's left nostril.

The heavy lurched back onto the floor but The Mole kept the barrel in position forcing the Muppet back up against the wall.

Then The Mole twisted the gun around in his hand so the small metal sight at the end of the barrel nicked the inside of this geezer's nostril. He winced with pain.

Then he pulled the nozzel out. The Muppet crumpled.

Jimmy The Mole's smile grew wider. He took a silencer out of his case and calmly screwed it onto the barrel.

"What the fuck ...?" I said.

The Mole ignored me and pointed the gun right at this bastard's head.

"This is out of order," I said, moving towards him.

The Mole turned and pointed the Glock straight at me.

"Shut it!"

The Mole then swung round again to face the Muppet but then aimed the gun to the floor and shot into his ankle.

Muppet man went rigid with pain and howled like a cat with a red-hot poker up its arse.

I smelt the cordite wafting across the room.

The silence that followed was deafening, if you

know what I mean.

Then The Mole screeched.

"Come on, Tone!"

We turned, ran out of the office and headed to the car. No one tried to stop us.

Once we were well away and clearly not being pursued, I slammed the brakes on and screeched to a halt in the middle of a built-up area.

That's when I had a right dig at Jimmy The Mole.

"Why the fuck're you packin' a piece?"

I prodded him in the shoulder as I yelled.

"Someone coulda got killed back there ..." I continued.

"Yeah, us" he screamed back. "We're dealin' with scum. Shooters are the only weapons they respect."

"You're a fuckin' lunatic," I said, stating the obvious.

"I don't give a fuck!"

We lapsed back into an awkward silence after that but he knew I was steaming mad about that shooter.

I was just turning right off the Valance Road when The Mole started talking again.

"Now, what were you sayin' about my little girl," he said.

"You give me that shooter and I'll tell you what's happenin'."

"Get fucked."

"I don't work with guns. Never have. Never will."

"But we need protection."

"I got me own weapon," I said, holding up my right fist.

"It's not like the old days, Tony," he said, trying to sound calm. "Everyone carries a piece these days."

"Well, I ain't everyone."

Then something very bloody surprising happened. He handed me the shooter without mentioning another word about it. A couple of seconds later the Mole asked me, "So where is she?"

"With that piece of shit Anif."

"Where?"

I told The Mole all about what I'd seen at the firing range and then the meeting in the church.

We couldn't do anything that evening so I offered to take The Mole home.

"Tomorrow's goin' to be a long day," I said.

24

I didn't usually get back to The Mole's place in Islington mid evening so it seemed a bit strange struggling through the trafficky streets.

All that anger from the boozer had gradually subsided. I didn't even feel any real hatred towards the old boy or the Muppet. I even wished I hadn't hit that old bastard so bloody hard.

But that punch-up had a profound effect on The Mole and me. And the way he handed me his shooter seemed to imply he completely trusted me. Now we were more like a team. Or at least that's how I felt.

By the time we got to The Mole's street he was slumped asleep in the passenger seat beside me. I was just about to sling the Merc up when I spotted something.

I braked suddenly, stirring The Mole in the process.

"What's going on?" he said wearily squinting into the darkness.

"See that Beemer there?"

He looked over at where I was pointing. It was a red 5 series BMW parked just near the entrance to his flats.

"What about it?"

"I reckon it's Anif's car."

"You sure?"

"I been followin' one like it all afternoon."

"How'd he know where I live?"

"Benny ..."

I accelerated away and took a left turn.

"It might belong to someone in the street," said The Mole. "You don't know for sure, do you?"

I took another left, and drove slowly until I came back to Essex Road again. Then I stopped and let the engine idle.

"It bloody well looked like his motor to me" I said.

"Look, we're jumpin' all over the place here," replied The Mole. "There must be thousands of cars like that."

"So, you wanna go back?" I asked.

"Yes."

I drove along the main Essex Road, then turned back into his street. A parking place had appeared outside the block of flats so I pulled up to it. That same Beemer was still there.

"Want a bevvy?" asked The Mole before getting out of the car.

"Yeah, alright."

After I'd locked the Merc we walked to the main doors of the flats. I turned and checked out the street one last time while he got his keys out.

Inside we waited for the lift and he asked: "Haven't you got a bird to sort out, then?"

"Wish I had."

The lift arrived and once we were inside The Mole closed the criss-cross iron gates and turned to me.

"I never played away from home while I was married but now I'd give anything for a kiss an' a cuddle."

"I know what you mean."

The lift was slowly rising, creaking on its ancient mountings. The Mole was still nodding his head in agreement with what I'd just said.

Then the lift stopped with a jerk that almost made us lose our footing. The Mole pulled the lift gate back and we stepped onto the landing.

Anif was there.

The Mole yelled. Anif moved towards us at top speed with his eyes flaring. His arm swung from low down, like a rising punch but in his huge fist was the gleaming blade of an open razor. The fist slashed at The Mole's face, aiming at his eyes.

I dived in front of him, trying to deflect him. But he still got through. The blade missed The Mole's face by centimetres and sliced through my forearm.

I howled, with shock more than pain, but I still smashed hard into Anif and he completely lost his balance.

As he fell to the floor I kicked out and caught him

right in the balls. He hardly flinched and jumped to his feet again. Then I threw a punch at his face but completely missed and he grabbed me.

As Anif swung around, I managed to get free of him.

"In the lift!" I yelled, but The Mole was already there.

I scrambled after him, slammed the iron gate closed and held it there as Anif tried to force it open and stab the razor through the bars. The Mole punched the button and we slowly started sinking.

As the lift went down we could see Anif running down the concrete steps around us.

Blood was gushing from my arm and I tried to hold it tightly to me.

"You all right?" The Mole said.

I nodded my head but said nothing.

The slow-moving lift reached the landing below when Anif leapt into sight, roaring with rage and furiously shaking the gate.

The Mole and I ducked back as Anif's nine-inch razor slashed at the air in front of us.

The lift continued its painfully slow journey. Once again we heard the familiar sound of Anif's feet racing down the steps.

And, naturally, he was there to greet us at the next landing, waiting to try and snatch open the gate as the lift passed. I stood back and kicked at his hand on the lift door with my shoe. It forced him to pull his hand back.

The lift continued downwards. Anif followed. We

could hear him throughout. We could also feel him around us.

I then whispered to The Mole: "Stop the lift."

"Why?"

"Just do it."

We were between floors and Anif was somewhere very nearby. The Mole jabbed desperately at the emergency stop button. The car halted with an almighty lurch that nearly knocked us off our feet.

Then there was total silence.

"Where is he?" The Mole said.

I raised a finger to my lips, and whispered: "Listen."

Suddenly we heard footsteps, but they weren't like earlier. Anif was creeping somewhere behind us, on the stairs, or on one of the landings.

I crouched down slowly, trying to hold my sliced arm against my chest. Blood was seeping onto the front of my shirt.

The floor of the lift car was just a few inches below the ceiling of the landing beneath us. Easing forward, I tried to peer out, but the view was restricted. Anif might be there, just a few inches away, out of sight, waiting with his hand on the catch of the door, ready to snatch it open as we passed.

The Mole, back against the rear wall of the car, didn't look happy.

"Is he there?" he whispered.

I shook my head, trying to reassure him, but I didn't really have a fucking clue and I was so wound up my head kept wobbling back and forward, shuddering.

I looked down and noticed my blood lying in

streaks and pools all over the floor.

Footsteps again. Soft, almost gentle, somewhere behind us.

I looked up.

Anif was above us. I could see him through the upper few inches of the gate.

"Tony!"

I dived at the buttons, punching every one at the same time. The lift groaned into action, and started going down once more.

But Anif, crouching above us, then hurled a bottle into the car. It smashed on the wall next to The Mole. He just managed to duck away from it.

I shouted to him: "Yell!"

"What?"

"Your eyes ... he hit your eyes!"

The Mole looked at me blankly for a split second then finally got it. The screaming would distract Anif. It might make him think he'd done some damage. It might also attract attention, something Anif certainly wouldn't want. The combination of thinking he'd done his job and not wanting to be seen might drive him off. On the other hand it might just make us look a right couple of twats, but, what the fuck, it was worth a go. The Mole yelled, drew breath and yelled again. It wasn't even worthy of the Parkhurst amateur dramatics society but in the circumstances it would do.

The lift continued its painfully slow journey. We could still hear Anif running down the steps alongside us.

I leaned against the gate, my hands resting on the buttons, watching the landings slip past us. When we got to the halfway mark I hit the stop button again. I could hear Anif moving somewhere above us.

I waited.

Then I pressed the button to take the lift up again.

"Keep it down!"

The Mole stopped his acting and stood behind me, breathing in short, sharp heavy rasps.

I let the lift get half up to the next floor and then stopped it again.

The whole building was silent. We both strained to hear anything.

Then I said quietly: "How far would you say it is to your door?"

"No more than twenty feet."

"Is there anywhere he could hide?"

"No." He was staring at the bloodstained floor. "Don't think so ... no, there ain't."

"You ready to give it a go?"

He shook his head.

"OK, then. Keep listening."

We waited for five minutes. It felt more like five hours. All the time the blood kept seeping down my arm into my clothes and then dripped onto the floor.

Then I said: "Right, here we go?"

He nodded.

I hit one of the buttons and the lift slowly sank. As we passed each landing we looked to either side and I was ready to kick out if Anif appeared.

We got to the bottom of the lift shaft, then rose again

to The Mole's floor. There was no sign of Anif anywhere.

I kept the lift quiet for a few minutes before carefully opening the gate. I could see down both ends of the corridor. No sight of anyone.

"You all right?" I asked The Mole.

"'Course."

"He's not here. Come on."

We stepped out of the blood-soaked lift and began moving towards her door.

Just then another door opened and a young woman came out. She slammed her door, then turned back to lock it.

I smiled and nodded to her. She glanced at me, spotted the blood and looked away.

At The Mole's door, he fumbled his keys, rattling them noisily against the lock.

My injured arm hung limply beside me, until the pressure made it throb with pain.

Once we got inside and the door was double locked I collapsed in a chair. He threw me a roll of bandage.

I took my jacket off, rolled up my torn shirtsleeve and wound the bandage around my arm.

It might have looked horrible but the wound wasn't that deep. I'd been lucky.

But my hand felt numb even though I could still use it. My arm felt sore and stiff but I knew it would be okay.

Meanwhile The Mole carefully searched the flat to make sure Anif hadn't somehow got inside. No sign.

Then The Mole fixed us both strong drinks.

We both knocked back that first drink quickly and then he refilled the glasses and sat down opposite me. He got up again almost immediately and went to the window, parted the curtains a fraction of an inch and peered down the street.

"Any sign of him?" I asked The Mole.

"Can't see him."

"What about the car?"

"I'm not sure."

I moved to his side.

"It's gone ... if that was the one."

"One thing's for sure."

"What?"

"He'll be back."

Then The Mole started prowling the room touching objects, as if sensing they were about to be taken away from him; his life was changing, being forced to change.

"We gotta get outta here," I said.

"I worked that one out," replied The Mole.

"You could stay at my mate's place. It's down by the river. My mate, Carl. He's quite a character."

"I don't like characters."

"You'd like Carl."

He shook his head.

"No ... I'll get a room. Somewhere out of the way."

"Like where?"

"The Westbury."

"What's that ... a hotel?"

"Yeah. But they owe me a favour."

I looked at him with contempt.

"That's a clever move."

"What d'you mean?"

"Bed down at a hotel that knows your line of business. Why not take a full page ad out in The Sun?"

I took a long, deep breath.

"It seems to me that for once in your life you gotta do whatever the fuck I say."

I pulled up in the garage next to Carl's flat, then took The Mole's bag from the boot.

"Is this it?" he asked.

I ignored him and led him round to the door on the street and we walked along a dark corridor that led to the steps to the upstairs flat.

As we walked in there was a sudden movement from the far end of the flat. A beautiful, ebony-skinned girl in her mid-twenties was standing completely stark bollock naked looking at us. The Mole's eyes nearly popped out his sockets. Just then, Carl appeared behind her with a towel around his waist. We didn't need any introductions.

"Sheeba. Say 'allo ta my friend Tony."

Sheeba giggled and ran back into Carl's bedroom.

"Carl, this is The Mole. The Mole, Carl."

They nodded uneasily at each other.

"Nice to meet you."

"Where am I going to sleep?" said The Mole.

25

I waited until I was really sure. Being sure was a feeling I knew well, one that had got me through the bad times in the good and bad old days. It had even helped me survive in the slammer when things got out of hand.

It wasn't the same feeling as being certain about something; it was nothing to do with finding out facts. Sureness was a feeling inside me. It made me know that I was doing the right thing even if I was hanging around with the wrong faces.

I'd been brooding for too long about Benny and Anif and Jenny. It was time to do something about it. But first I had to be sure I'd got it all right. There was still plenty I didn't know about Benny's dealings, but at least I was now sure about who the good guys were.

That was easy, there was only one — me. It's pretty fucking lonely being a good guy.

My head was clearer than it had been in weeks, even months. It was like someone had chucked a bucket of cold water in my face and snapped me awake from a bad dream.

I could taste the excitement, even smell it rising out of my throat. My body was tensed up for action just like it always was before a big fight. It was great to get that feeling back. I felt on top of the world. Invincible. Ready to take on all comers.

You see, since getting out I'd even started to develop a new quality, if you want to call it that. My instinct for dealing with trouble, and the way to deal with it, had improved. Now I knew I was ready to deal with it all.

I slipped out of Carl's place without waking anyone, and drove east towards Chigwell, in what I used to call "my part of Essex."

Besides me, on the passenger seat, and concealed inside an ordinary paper bag, was the Glock 9mm I'd confiscated from Jimmy The Mole. By now you'll have realised how much I hate shooters but I needed some sort of protection for what I had planned.

And you don't need to be a bloody rocket scientist to know what was going to happen the next time I came across that bastard Anif.

Or Benny for that matter.

Benny was the main man. Anif did the legwork, but Benny pulled the strings.

I drove across Chigwell Heath and down through

the small sidestreets on the south side without even having to pause to look at my A-Z. It was 12 years since I'd been here, but it felt like yesterday.

I even remembered the parking routine near Benny's place. He'd told me once: "Don't park up too near the house, Tone. Much better to sling your motor in that little lane round the back."

Benny didn't like me making myself too obvious when I popped over to Chigwell. I never worked out if it was because he didn't want to upset the neighbours or because he liked to keep me at a distance.

So much for being in the family. In those days I was nothing more than a piece of profitable meat for him. A piece of meat he could reheat over and over again until I got past my sell-by date.

The little lane was still there. It was more like a pathway for horses and walkers going on to the heath than I remembered. But there was plenty of parking space. Twenty yards away there was access to the main road: a quick left turn, another to the right, and I'd be on a fast dual carriageway back up west.

I got a bit of a surprise when I spotted another motor already there. It was a large 7 series white BMW. I stopped the Merc in front of it, deliberately blocking it in.

Then I checked the shooter carefully. I released the box magazine, and made sure the firing mechanism was working. Just because I don't like shooters doesn't mean I don't know how to use one. Then I slotted the clip back in its place. It looked fairly new. Hopefully that meant it wouldn't jam ... but I knew I'd have to watch the recoil.

"Use both hands and aim low," was the advice I'd got from my cousin Tommy 15 years earlier — the only other time I'd ever handled a shooter.

"Go for the balls and you'll get him in the heart."

I'd been visiting Tommy at his home near Dallas, Texas, at the time. He owned a shooting range out in the sticks and I can tell you it was one of the scariest days of my life.

I hadn't been keen on even holding a shooter let alone using it, but Tommy convinced me it was worth a crack. So he gave me a three-minute crash course with a 9mm Glock and then plonked me in the range with a pair of headphones over my ears.

I banged off half a dozen bullets and every one hit the target in the area around the heart. Then I started shaking. I put the piece down and the waft of cordite stung my nostrils. I told Tommy I'd never let off another shooter as long as I lived.

"Don't like it, Tom. Makes me nervous. It's too bloody dangerous."

"But you're real good at it," he replied.

"That's why it's not for me, old son."

So here I was, 15 years later, slipping an almost identical Glock into my inside pocket. The safety catch on the trigger was still on.

Then I walked towards the immaculate redbrick wall alongside the left side of Benny's totally over-the-top electronically operated ornate black metal gates that opened into the grounds of the house.

Luckily I knew that — like many other major dodgepots this side of Hoxton — Benny didn't keep guard dogs despite signs to the contrary on his fancy front gate. Benny was more of a pussy man, really.

Anyway, I popped over the wall and strolled through the undergrowth and trees until I had a clear view of his house. It was late afternoon and the orange autumn sun was just starting to dip behind the roof.

Benny's place was a big Edwardian villa, with towers at each end and leaded windows. It looked a bit like something out of the Addams Family. There was a long patio between the two main wings of the house. It all looked quite tasteful until you got close up. Then you realised it was all a bit fake.

I found a perfect spot in the bushes to wait and watch. I had a clear view with good cover.

Then there was some movement. A light came on in the room that opened onto the main patio, and Benny appeared in view. He was at the French windows, then drew the curtains moments before the lights were switched off.

A few seconds later I noticed the curtains moving and then the glass door to the patio slid open. Benny walked out, and closed the door behind him.

He stood on the patio for a few seconds, glancing around the garden but he wasn't looking for anything special. He was togged up in a dinner jacket with a bow tie. Then he reached inside his suit jacket, took out a big cigar and lit it.

He seemed happy as Larry puffing away. One hand

was slipped inside his jacket pocket, the other holding the cigar.

Then Benny walked slowly round the garden towards one of the wings of the house: he took out a ring of keys from his pocket, let himself in and closed the door behind him.

I waited another couple of minutes then left my hiding place and walked briskly across the lawn. I knew there was a risk I'd be spotted if anyone was looking out of the house but it didn't seem likely.

I felt all right. I wasn't afraid. But then I did have that shooter burning a hole in my pocket.

The French door Benny had originally come out of was unlocked and I slipped quietly inside. I hadn't been there in 12 years so I got quite a shock. It was decked out like a torture chamber.

On one wall was a thick pair of dark red velvet curtains and facing these were a number of chairs. A small hi-tech video camera was mounted on a tripod, pointing towards the curtains, and some other cameras lay around the floor. I walked to the curtains and snatched them open.

Bright light poured in on me through a glass wall. On the other side of the glass, obviously a two-way mirror was a room Benny no doubt called his amusement arcade. I'd call it his insurance policy. The area behind the glass was fitted out like a fantasy room in a pricey brothel: a huge bed, a bath, several long tables with padded tops ... all arranged so they were in clear view of the cameras. The ceiling was mirrored, naturally, as were the walls.

Benny was fully equipped to supply every bit of filth and degradation you could imagine. I pulled open the cupboards to find they were full of rubber, leather, plastic, you name it. On one wall were loads of whips, thongs, chains, ropes, leather masks and rubber and even crystal glass dildos and other monster things people shove up their arses.

Then I saw two people walk into the room behind the glass. They came in from separate doors.

It was Jenny — and she was with a client.

He was past middle-age, overweight and balding. He was also completely starkers. He turned around and pulled Jenny into his arms and started manhandling her. She was dressed in a flimsy, white see-through dress.

The man turned her around and began rubbing himself against her from behind, his arms wrapped around her stomach, bending her forward. Trying to get his hands lower.

I found it hard to watch as he pushed himself harder and harder against her. Now he was right up against the two-way mirror, distorting her features as he thrust into her. Her nose and lips were warped like rubber against the glass.

Then he pushed her head down and it scraped the glass. Now she was crouching. Her pale, young skin left scuff marks on the smooth glass. When he got her into the position he wanted, the man ripped at her dress and then tore down her panties.

Then he entered her forcefully from behind, jerking and thrusting. Seeing the look of pain on her face got me really angry. I couldn't just stand by and watch this.

Jenny's face was contorted. She was crying. I kept seeing my own kid's face. Her eyes were glazed, her mouth hung open limply. She was hardly breathing. Her arms dropped loosley by her side like a rag doll. Her eyelids drooped.

Then the man pulled back, leaving Jenny's features warped against the mirror. She didn't move for a few seconds. It was almost as if she was frozen in time.

The man (I don't even feel happy calling him one) then moved towards one of the padded tables where two or three flat dishes were laid down. There was a glint of something in them. They seemed to contain sweets.

Or capsules of drugs.

Then this sick bastard picked up a hypodermic syringe and began screwing a phial into it. He raised the syringe to the light like some nutty professor and squirted a thin jet of liquid into the air.

I had to act fast. There was a door at the side of the two-way mirror, concealed from those inside the room, and Jenny was leaning next to it. I watched as this horrible old man turned and moved alongside her.

Then I pushed open the door and caught him right in the head. He went flying. I grabbed him off the floor and nutted him with all my strength. I wanted him to really suffer. He crumbled instantly back onto the floor.

Jenny was leaning against the wall. She slumped into my arms.

I pulled her into the anteroom. Back in the main room, that sick old bastard was writhing and moaning on the floor.

I slapped Jenny gently on the cheeks: "You awake?"

"'Course I am." She turned and faced me, but her eyelids were still drooping, and her head wouldn't stay up.

"Can you walk?"

She nodded. "Gissa hand," she said but her words were slurred and her attention kept wandering. "Who are you?"

"Never mind all that. Get your knickers on."

They were still tangled round her ankles and she just managed to bend down and pull them up. Then she smoothed down her paper-thin dress as if she was trying to rub something off that was sticking to her palm.

Inside the room, I noticed the man was grappling at his clothes, trying to put them on. He then ripped open the door and began shouting to someone outside.

"We gotta go," I said to the girl.

I carried her towards the door to the garden and pushed her through it. Then I grabbed her and ran her across the lawn. Jenny, barefoot and weak, kept stumbling, and weaving from side to side.

"I know you," she said suddenly.

"Shut up and keep running!"

"What you doin' here?"

"I'm from ..."

But I didn't get a chance to say anything more because she then tripped, and I had to haul her to her feet. Behind us, Benny had appeared on the patio.

He shouted: "Tony! What the fuck ..?"

"Come on!" I yelled, desperately pulling her along by the arm. By this time we'd hit a tangle of bushes and when I looked back I couldn't see Benny any more.

We reached the car. I bundled the girl into the passenger seat, slammed the door shut and ran round to the driver's side.

Thank fuck, the engine fired up first time and I shot off, kicking up a shower of soil, stones and dead leaves behind us.

I saw Benny in my rear view as he appeared in the lane behind us, panting and coughing. He stood there long enough to note the car. When I glanced back a last time he was kicking the stones with anger.

Then he turned and headed back towards the house.

26

Iknew we'd be followed so I drove as fast as I could without alerting Old Bill's interest in the process.

Once we'd got clear of London I swung onto a country A road and drove quickly through a couple of villages. Then we stopped in an entrance to a field to make doubly certain we didn't have a tail.

When no other motors appeared, I carried on through the back roads until I swung back onto the main A road and slowed up a bit.

Jenny was flat out most of the time. Her head kept lolling back on the seat and her eyes remained closed. Her mouth hanging half open and her lips glistened with spittle. Her hands fell limply in her lap.

When she wasn't dozing, she was fretting about in the seat, unable to keep still for more than a second.

Then she'd just as suddenly slump back in her seat again.

She couldn't answer any of my questions and when I tried to tell her I was working for her dad she just snorted and shut her eyes. After a while I just gave up and kept on driving.

Jenny looked innocent and childlike when she was asleep and her dress could have come off a twelve-year-old it was so small. But her eyes — when they were open — were the things that gave her away. They were watery, old, unhappy, glazed and shifty.

The nails on her hands were broken and bitten to the quick. Her bony knuckles were virtually red-raw and her skin seemed almost green in colour. And she exposed her breasts every time she moved in the car seat, which didn't exactly make me feel too comfortable.

Once back on the main road, I noticed Jenny became a little more alert. She even sat upright in the seat and looked out at the passing countryside. Then she glanced at me.

"So he sent you to kidnap me."

"What?" I said.

"My so-called dad," She said it like a teenage girl who's just been grounded for staying out after midnight.

"He was worried about you."

"Sure he was," she replied, before slumping back asleep.

About ten minutes later she woke up again.

"Not much of a job is it?" Her voice sounded calm,

despite everything that had just happened.

"What you on about?" I replied.

"You know ... breaking into houses."

"How else am I supposed to spring a damsel in distress?" I said, immediately realising how stupid that must have sounded.

"They'll come after me ..." Jenny said.

I took my eyes off the road and looked across at her. Her watery pupils were struggling to focus.

"... you'll see," she said.

I hoped to hell she'd be proved wrong.

Then she dropped her head forward and started crying. The tears rolled down her cheeks, smudging her black eye makeup. I reached behind and pulled a box of Kleenex off the back window ledge and dropped them in her lap. She blew her nose, then tossed the crumpled tissue out the window.

"Anif will be so angry" she said.

"Why?"

"I belong to him."

"You don't belong to no one."

"He'll kill us both."

"Not if he can't find us, he won't."

She looked back over her shoulder at the road behind, making me glance quickly in the rear-view mirror. We still seemed to be in the clear.

"Can't you drive a bit fuckin' faster?" she said, suddenly sounding like a tough street-wise hustler again.

I ignored her.

Jenny stayed awake for a few more silent minutes.

Then the drugs took over again and her head slumped back on the headrest. I carried on driving.

Just outside Clacton I slowed the car down, signalled left, and drove into the car park of a Little Chef. It was virtually empty.

I got out and looked around.

Inside the Merc, Jenny stirred. I walked back to her.

She said: "I'm hungry."

"We gotta wait here."

"Why?"

"Your dad's on his way."

"Great," she said sarcastically. "I really want to see him."

"Don't be daft. He's gonna sort you out."

"Sort me out?" She paused. "I don't like being sorted out."

"What d'you mean?"

"Nothin'."

"He just wants to help you back on the straight and narrow."

"Where's that then?" she responded. It was a good point.

Then she changed tactics.

"I told you, I'm hungry."

I opened the car door for her and she got out. The loose gravel cut into her naked feet and she almost lost her balance for a moment. I caught her arm to support her, and as I did her loose fitting dress slipped down from one shoulder exposing most of her breast.

I tried to pull the dress back up.

"Can't you button it up or something?"

"Could do," she grinned at me and I realised the other side of her was never far away. The grin broadened even more. She let her head drop slightly to one side then looked right at me.

"You wanna do it with me, don't you?"

"Give it a rest."

"You fancy doin' it with a young bird. You're all the fuckin' same."

"Do your dress up please, Jenny."

For a moment she looked almost disappointed. She picked awkwardly at the buttons with her fingers, but that simply made her go off balance again and I had grab hold of her again.

"What drugs did that old bastard feed you?" I asked her.

"Who cares?"

"Don't you know what they were?"

She shook her head vaguely.

I led her into the Little Chef, and we went to a booth by the window that overlooked the car park. Jenny slumped in her seat, draping her thin arms across the tabletop and playing idly with the sugar in the bowl. I found myself staring at the tattoo on the back of her hand.

"D'you like it?" she asked. I immediately wished I'd never looked at it.

"No," I said.

Then I asked her: "Why d'you have it done?"

She didn't respond.

"... musta hurt like hell."

"I've had worse."

Then she raised her arm, squinted at the tattoo, and smiled.

"Did it for Anif," she said beaming emptily.

"You did it for that bastard?"

"He's a better bastard than most."

She traced the inner heart with a fingertip, then the outer one.

"This was me, this was him. I love him."

The waitress came to the table, holding a small order pad.

"What can I do for you?" she said.

"Yeah ... I'll have steak and chips, and a cuppa tea, please. What about you?" I said to Jenny.

"Ice cream."

"Thought you wanted to eat somethin'?"

"That's all I can eat."

"What flavour?" asked the waitress.

"Whatever you got."

The waitress didn't know how to handle Jenny's reply so I came to the rescue.

"Give her a scoop of vanilla, chocolate and strawberry."

"Don't like strawberry," mumbled Jenny.

The waitress was looking at me like I was some dirty old man out on a date with a schoolgirl.

"Make it just chocolate and vanilla."

The waitress huffed, scribbled down the order and walked away.

As she walked off, I turned back to Jenny.

"What d'you mean it's all you can eat?" I asked her.

"It's all I can eat."

"What does that mean?"

"You know."

"No, I don't bloody know," I said, remembering that other street kid Lorna and the last time I'd been in a caff with her.

"Can't eat proper food no more. Not real food."

I didn't know what to say so I just shook my head. She looked at me very seriously then, frowning.

"You don't know much, do you?"

"No ... I don't," I said, shaking my head.

The waitress returned with the ice cream, and Jenny wolfed it down.

"Don't mind me," I said as it dribbled down the side of her mouth.

Once she'd finished she pushed the empty bowl away and then squinted right into my eyes.

"You're pretty cool, you know," she said.

I looked at her and arched my eyebrows.

"D'you rate me, then?"

"Don't know you, do I?" I said.

27

Jenny stared silently at her empty ice cream bowl as I finished my meal and supped at my tea.

People in the caff were looking at her, especially blokes, just like they had done when I'd been with young Lorna. I just hoped they thought Jenny was my daughter.

But if she had been my kid I can guarantee she wouldn't have got mixed up in this sort of shit. Not if I'd been around. That then got me thinking about Karen yet again.

It wasn't until a car crunched across the gravel outside that I snapped out of thoughts. My best mate Carl was at the wheel.

Glancing at Jenny, I could see she'd already noticed her dad in the passenger seat. She didn't look very pleased.

I said to her: "Wait here."

I moved outside quickly, and got there in time to open the door for Jimmy The Mole.

"Well done," he said to me, brushing past me towards the caff.

Carl climbed out the other side, and leaned against the side of the car.

"Hope yo doin' de right ting," he said.

"So do I."

I turned and looked through the caff window where Jimmy The Mole was leaning over Jenny, wrapping his arms around the girl's neck and shoulders, stroking her hair and pressing her face to his shoulders.

Jenny seemed in even more of a daze than before, and it bothered me the way she stared blankly out of the window throughout.

Every now and again, The Mole glanced out at me. Then turned his head back to Jenny.

"Wot d'you reckon?" Carl said, nodding towards them.

"Your guess is as good as mine. I just did what I was asked."

Carl said: "Wot's all dis really about, Tony?"

"It's complicated."

"More complicated dan yo' life story?"

"Much more."

"Yo never learn, do ya?" said Carl.

28

Carl headed back to the smoke and about half an hour later I found myself driving slowly along the seafront at Clacton, weaving through the heavy traffic. It was already getting dark and I was knackered.

The Mole and Jenny were in the back of the Merc. Jenny was asleep with her head resting on her father's shoulder.

"So, what do we do now?" I said over my shoulder to him.

"I'm thinkin'," whispered The Mole, so as not to wake his kid.

A long silence followed. At one stage I tipped the rear-view to see what was going on. Nothing. Nada. The Mole was staring out of the window at the sea.

Jenny had woken up and was looking out in the opposite direction.

Then at last he said: "Let's find an hotel."

"Which one?"

"You decide."

"What do we want? Posh? Cheap? What?"

"That one'll do," said The Mole, pointing out an old Victorian building on the town side of the seafront road.

"Posh," I muttered under my breath as I swung the motor across a gap in the central reservation and bumped it up the ramp into the hotel set-down area.

The Mole and Jenny got out and then a snotty looking commissionaire told me I'd have to take the car to the underground car park.

A few minutes later, I strolled into the hotel reception and found The Mole and Jenny waiting for me. She looked bloody awful, like she was about to keel over. The Mole told me he couldn't hold her up much longer.

"I'll take her," I said. "You bring the luggage."

"Luggage?" The Mole asked.

"Only jokin'," I said.

I slipped an arm around Jenny's waist, and then draped one of her own arms around my neck. The hotel staff didn't look too happy as I carried her to the lift.

The Mole told me he'd booked two rooms next to each other: a single and a double. He opened the door of the double, and I pulled Jenny in and across to one of the beds.

Her eyes then opened briefly.

"Where is he?" she mumbled.

"Who?"

Just then The Mole chipped in: "I'm here, sweetheart. Don't worry, I'm here."

Jenny turned her head, looked up at me quizzically and then blearily across at The Mole.

"Who's this, dad?"

"This is Tony. He's ..."

"Oh I remember. Tony the ice cream man. Your van's outside. I can hear the music playing."

She started laughing in a high, hysterical giggly voice. Then she hiccupped and began choking before snorting a load of green shit out of her nose.

"Bloody hell! We gotta get her sorted out."

The Mole moved into the bathroom and came back with some tissues and started cleaning her up. She then lay back on the bed chuckling to herself.

"Tony the ice cream man. Ding, ding, ding ..."

I picked up one of her hands trailing down towards the floor and folded it over her chest.

"She's burnin' hot," I said.

"I know," said The Mole placing his palm on Jenny's forehead.

Jenny was struggling on the bed as if she was tied up when she wasn't. The Mole held her down, pressing on both her shoulders to keep her flat on the bed. Then he wiped her forehead with a damp white flanel.

"We gotta get a doc or somethin'," I said.

"There'll be a chemist open somewhere.' said The

Mole. Will you do me a favour?"

"What?"

The Mole released Jenny for a few moments, and reached across to the bedside table for the folder of hotel notepaper. He scribbled something on a sheet, and passed it to me.

"Go and get this, will ya?"

"What is it?"

"The chemist'll know what it is."

"I hope he can read it."

"Just get your skates on, Tony."

I wanted to ask him how come he knew what she needed but now wasn't the time or the place. The Mole looked pretty serious at that moment.

When I got to the door I looked across at him. He was back dabbing his daughter's forehead. I was just opening the door when I had second thoughts.

"There's somethin' you'd better have," I said to him.

"What?"

"Just in case." I reached into my pocket, and pulled out the shooter. "Never know, do you?"

He took it from me and balanced it in his hand. He looked even more serious.

"You reckon they'll find us?"

"They could do."

Jimmy The Mole bent his head, looked at the gun and then across at that helpless little girl on the bed.

As I left the room I saw The Mole slipping the gun under the spare pillow on the bed.

It took me nearly an hour to find a chemist up the hill

near the railway station. The assistant gave me the drugs after rabbiting at length with the duty pharmacist.

She even asked me: "D'you know how to administer this correctly?"

"Yeah ... course I do."

I walked quickly back to the hotel, keeping an eye out for any unwelcome visitors.

Just to be on the safe side I even took the lift up to the floor below the rooms in case I was being followed. I took the emergency stairs to the rooms.

I let myself in expecting The Mole to be angry at how long it had taken me to get the medicine.

Instead the room was deathly quiet.

The only light came from a small lamp just inside the door. The Mole was sitting at a table by the window while Jenny was flat out on the bed.

She was either alseep or unconscious.

The Mole made no attempt to turn and say hello even though he knew I was there.

After a few seconds I said: "I bought the medicine." The Mole didn't flicker an eyelid. So I said: "I'll leave it here for you."

"Thanks, mate," he mumbled. Then he raised his face and looked across at me. "Thanks."

29

I sat and watched telly for a couple of hours in my room but I couldn't tell you what was on. Then I got restless and went out. I found a pub in the market area and stayed there knocking back halves of lager until closing time. But I still felt as sober as a judge when I walked back to the hotel.

I knew if I went up to my room I'd just lie there brooding about everything so I went down to the beach.

I clattered across the shingle to the water's edge. I took off my shoes and socks and let the cold water lap across my toes. It felt soothing.

Then I turned my back to the waves and looked at the town. The street lights looked blurry, and the noise of the traffic was drowned out by the sea as it swept in and out of the beach.

I turned round again and took a long piss on the shingle, watching the luminous waves breaking and roaring towards me.

It was the first time I'd been in the sea for twelve long years and here I was pissing into it. I should have known better. I started thinking again about The Mole and Jenny.

Then I strolled along the beach for a while dragging my feet in the frothy sea and shingle until I reached a rundown pier. I stood beneath the walkway, looking up at the dark monster shape above me and looked along it until it reached the sea. Barnacles crusted the metal legs and black, old, shiny seaweed made it slimy to touch.

That's when I remembered the last time I'd been in Clacton. Must have been nearly 20 years ago. Back then Benny fancied himself as the Don King of the East End. After one of my biggest wins against a man mountain called Terry Hall from Rotherhithe, Benny brought me and a couple of his other big hitters to Clacton for a weekend off.

We all went on the pier and he encouraged us to go on the Dodgem cars, shoot pennies on arcade games and wear silly seaside hats. Benny played at being the father figure with nothing more than our interests at heart. Believe that and you'd fucking well believe anything.

As it happened, on that particular night in Clacton, a watchman was shot during an armed robbery of a factory on the outskirts of town. He didn't die. But some of Benny's "associates" were in the frame for it. It made Clacton a hot place for a while. So we never went back after that.

Later I heard he only took us to Clacton because he had a meet with his "associates" before they carried out the blagging and he wanted a decent alibi.

Benny had always been good at picking up new members for his so-called family. That made me wonder where he'd got that evil bastard Anif from? A psycho like him wouldn't have got within a mile of us in the old days.

Back then, Benny's interest in vice had been nothing more than a sideline. Of course, me and the other fighters in his stable had heard rumours about him running a team of pimps and their girls. But our minds were on the fight game so we never rocked the boat.

Walking back up the beach that night I realised Benny's Clacton blagging was the first time I'd got a direct sniff of some of his heavier criminal activities. The second time was when I took the rap for him. And that cost me twelve years of my life, as you already know.

Yet here I was about to get involved in the gunfight at the OK Corral in Clacton.

There were a few matters that required my careful consideration:

Jimmy The Mole claimed Anif could not know where he lived and he had seemed genuinely surprised when Anif turned up at his flat.

But Anif worked for Benny, so it wouldn't have been difficult for him to find out. Then again, it might have been the other way round. Maybe Benny worked for Anif. Unlikely, but possible. Anyway, they worked together. Henry and Del did work for Benny: they always had, and they were still up to mischief.

Henry had got me the driving job, the mobile phone ... and through the driving job I had been hired out to The Mole.

Henry knew The Mole, Benny knew The Mole ... and Anif always had, back when he first tried to find Jenny.

Coincidence, or was The Mole ultimately responsible for his daughter's fate? It would certainly explain why he felt so bad about it.

If Anif had known where The Mole was all along then I was being set up — used to keep tabs on The Mole but ultimately expendable. Benny had certainly asked me to spy on the Mole. Call me suspicious, but I don't think he meant all that bollocks about me being part of the family. Once bitten and all that shit, if you know what I mean.

Anyhow, the more I thought about it, the less I liked it and I could sense trouble brewing. Big trouble, probably mainly for me.

Meanwhile, Jimmy The Mole sat there like a ghost in that room looking like he was about to top himself. It all bothered me a lot. I let myself into my room and pressed an ear to the connecting wall. I couldn't hear a thing.

30

I really struggled to get to sleep that night. Tossing and turning. Every time I nodded off something in my dreams forced me awake again.

Then I'd heard noises from a nearby room. Not bad noises, just low key voices. It could have been Jimmy The Mole and his kid. On the other hand, it might have been from another room. That went on until about four in the morning when I finally dozed off.

Broad daylight was peeping through the gap in the curtains when I was eventually woken by a knock on the door.

My eyes squinted as I opened them because the sun was reflecting in my face off a mirror over the dressing table. It gave me quite a shock when I saw my reflection. I looked bloody awful.

Then the knocking on the door came again.

"Hold on. Hold on," I shouted, as I grabbed a towel off the end of the bed. Expecting it to be a chambermaid, I pulled open the door.

It was Jimmy The Mole. He was fully dressed, and had his brief case in his hand.

"Fancy a walk by the seaside?"

I was still squinting and rubbing my eyes.

"What?"

"We gotta lot to sort out, me old son."

I didn't much like the happy tone of his voice.

I rubbed my hand over my bristly chin. "Gimme five minutes and I'm all yours."

But instead of leaving the room he walked in.

"What about Jenny next door?" I jerked a thumb towards the next room.

"She's asleep."

Jimmy The Mole nodded to himself but he didn't say anything more.

Twenty minutes later the two of us were strolling along the promenade in warm sunshine. The weather had brought out the crowds, even though it was almost the end of the season. I half expected to find people in deckchairs, fully clothed, with hankies on their heads. Instead I spotted two teenage girls sunbathing topless.

"Bloody hell, look at that!" I said.

The Mole glanced at what I was pointing at and laughed.

"That's a bit much, ain't it?" I said.

"It's only as nature intended," said The Mole.

"Just as long as they ain't too young," I replied.

Then I glanced up at the sun.

"Twelve years ... that's how long it's been. I could do with a bloody suntan."

Then we got to the entrance of the main pier on the seafront.

"What we gonna do next?" he asked as we started walking along the rickety wooden surface of the pier.

"That's up to you. I've done my bit."

"What d'you say?"

"I said I've done my bit and I'm out of here."

"What's your problem?" he said.

"What's my problem?" I said. "My problem is I've kidnapped your smackhead kid from a Turkish psycho pimp who's probably heading up a search party as we speak. I call that a problem."

"They'll never find us."

"Really? This isn't a fuckin' milkround or a bit of booze an' fags business. We're dealin' with some right hard bastards ..."

"You'll get some money, I promise," said The Mole.

"You think everythin's about fuckin' money, don't ya? I don't want to end up banged up or back on my toes. I want a normal life."

"Then why d'you walk back into Benny's firm?"

I couldn't be bothered to answer him so I stopped at a stall flogging the sort of jewellery I thought my kid Karen might like. The Mole trailed away from me, and went to stand at the rail on the promenade, staring down at the sea.

After buying Karen a ring, I walked back over to The Mole.

As we started walking along again I asked him, "So what's really the score with Jenny?"

The Mole frowned and looked up from a thousand thoughts.

"I shouldn't have got you involved," he said. "But I needed someone to find her for me."

Just then I noticed a teenage girl rowing with her mum and dad near us. I looked round at them. She was having a right dig at her old man.

I turned back to The Mole, who was watching the same scene.

"Doesn't matter what you do for them. They always give you a lot of grief, right?"

"Yeah," said The Mole.

"You ever have any really heavy duty dust-ups with Jenny?" I asked.

"Yeah. A few," The Mole said.

A look of irritation seemed to flicker across his face after he'd spoken.

"D'you ever give her a slappin'?"

"None of your fuckin' business."

I had to know so I carried on.

"Did you?" I asked again.

"She's my kid. She's all I got. That's it."

The expression on his face told me he was lost in his thoughts.

"Didn't you ever get angry with your kid?" asked The Mole.

"Never had the chance."

He nodded slowly.

"It hurts when they turn their backs on you," said The Mole.

I looked away from him and rested my elbows on the rail of the pier and stared blankly at the water. Couple of wetsuited beachboys on sea-scooters were thrashing about in the distance, throwing white foam into the air.

I heard the clicking of The Mole's fancy shoes as he walked slowly away from me. We were both lost in separate thoughts. He looked guilt-ridden. I was worried I might have just delivered him back the daughter he abused.

I was still watching those kids on their sea scooters riding the white horse out in the water.

Then, like a bolt out of the blue, The Mole yelled at the top of his voice.

"Fuckin' hell! Tony!"

I whirled round. The Mole was moving away from me, crouching in horror as he ran. Just beyond him, pushing violently through the crowds on the pier were three men.

Two of them were Henry and Del. Anif was in the lead, and he had a hand reaching for something in his inside pocket.

31

My eyes snapped around frantically trying to work out what direction I should head in. They were getting closer. The Mole had darted into the crowd opposite.

I reached into my pocket for the shooter and then remembered that I'd given it to The Mole and he'd left it under Jenny's pillow at the hotel.

"That way!" I yelled at him. "Come on!" I shouted even louder this time.

I caught up with The Mole, grabbed him by the scruff of his collar and spun him around before dragging him up the pier towards the amusement building.

We ran together to the end of the canopy. But he was struggling to keep up. We barged through the crowds. Then he tripped. I snatched at his arm, yanked him to his feet and made him keep running.

Anif was getting closer and closer and was only a few feet behind us by now. Then he paused, looked back and shouted something at the others before upping the tempo once more.

I looked across and saw Henry and Del running parallel with us on the other side of the pier. I reckoned they were planning to cut us off where the walkway broadened out further along.

We were really deep in the shit heading for a dead-end into the deep blue yonder. And we had no choice but to keep running and weaving through the crowds.

Just as Anif virtually caught up with me I crashed into a flower stall. I spun it around and shoved it in his direction. As he toppled off balance I saw the gun in his hand.

I scooped up a load of flowers and threw them right at him. But he was coming towards me with that shooter glistening in the sun.

I dived to one side but he knew which direction I was going in and aimed his gun right at me. The matt black barrel flashed in the sunlight. I could see his finger squeezing on the trigger.

I kicked out with all my strength and just managed to connect with his balls. He crumbled and the gun fell from his hand and clattered across the wooden walkway.

All around me people were screaming. As I backed away from Anif's doubled-up body, holidaymakers were pulled back from me in fear.

I spotted the gun on the floor and kicked it as hard as I could. It skidded across the boards and fell over the side into the sea just as Anif was getting to his feet, his face distorted with rage and pain.

I ran off in the direction The Mole was travelling only to spot Henry and Del holding him down on the ground. I went straight at Henry and popped him in the temple. He fell to the floor, releasing his grip on The Mole.

"Fuck off, Tony!" Del said. "We got no ruck with you."

"Well, you have now!" I screamed at them. "Come on! Let's have you!"

Then I raised my fists and moved in.

They backed off to consider their options, letting Jimmy The Mole move off again. I put my shoulder down and charged right at them, bouncing each to one side and thundering straight through between them.

I went through a bunch of people and headed for the exit turnstile with The Mole, who was only slightly ahead of me.

The three men were regrouping behind us. Anif was talking to the other two, standing up straight with his hands on his hips, flexing his back, like an athlete at the end of a race. Henry looked knackered, and was standing with his shoulders hunched, pressing his hand to the side of his head.

Del was pointing in our direction.

As I watched, the three of them started walking towards us once again. This time they were keeping it low key in an attempt to attract less attention.

Outside the pier, panting heavily, The Mole gasped at me: "What do we do now?"

"We get to my motor and drive the fuck outta here."

"What 'bout Jenny?"

"She's safe where she is."

"You're fuckin' kiddin'. They found us. They'll find her!"

"If we go back to the hotel they'll definitely bloody find her."

But despite it all we were both already walking in the direction of the hotel.

I looked behind us again and the three pricks were following at a distance but making no attempt to catch up with us.

I was huffing and puffing almost as badly as The Mole by this stage. I was slightly comforted by the thought of that shooter stashed away under the pillow back in The Mole's room.

"We'll give 'em somethin' to think about," I said. "Keep walkin' and do what I say. All right?"

For once The Mole agreed. He was in no fit shape to argue. We carried on past the hotel and then, when we were about a couple of hundred yards beyond it, I said to him: "Let's cross the road."

On the other side we continued walking briskly away from the hotel. The three men kept abreast of us on the other side of the road.

"See that bus," I mumbled to The Mole, nodding towards a green double-decker coming along the front in our direction. "We're going to get on it if it stops at the lights."

"What if it doesn't?"

"Then we get the next one."

Five minutes later we were a mile away in Clacton's main shopping area. There was no sign of our three new best friends. We hopped off the bus when I spotted a taxi, and got the driver to take us to the back entrance of the hotel.

Once we got in the hotel, everything seemed calmer.

In the lift I said to The Mole: "We pick up Jenny, then we get back to London, right?"

"Right."

But he didn't look happy.

We took the lift to the floor above the one with our rooms, then nipped down the emergency staircase. It was as quiet as stone in the corridor.

I turned to The Mole: "You got the key?"

The Mole nodded, and began rummaging around in his coat pocket. As he opened the door, I immediately smelt familiar cigar smoke.

Benny was there, sitting in an armchair next to the bed. He had the cigar perched delicately in one hand and in the other he had those white boxing gloves. Small grey tubes of cigar ash lay in a circle on the carpet around his feet.

He wasn't smiling, either.

Jenny was asleep on the bed, her pale tattooed hand tucked under her face like the paw of a snoozing kitten.

Me and The Mole both froze at the sight of him. Then The Mole moved towards his little girl.

"Ssh," said Benny, looking right at us. "We don't

want to wake her, do we?"

Then I started to say: "How the ...?"

"I told you to watch out for the little things, Tone."

"Leave it out, Benny," I said through gritted teeth.

"Leave it out? No, I don't think I can fuckin' leave it out." He stood up, and put the gloves down on the end of the bed where Jenny slept.

Then he walked around us both, and pushed the door shut.

"I've never taken the easy way out," he said to The Mole. "Not goin' to start now, neither."

I glanced at the bed, thinking of the gun that I presumed was in there somewhere near Jenny's head.

Benny was pacing around us, and he spotted the look on my face.

"You shoulda kept out of all this, Tone," he said. "A little scrubber gets hooked on smack, does a bit of s and m with a few clients of mine."

Then he turned on The Mole, and smashed the flat of his hand against his face.

"Clients you were trying to nick off me ..."

The Mole's face was turned sideways by the force of the blow. I could hear his breathing had become more strained.

Benny then took a fistful of The Mole's shirt, twisted it to get a good grip, and pulled him forward. Then he turned to me.

"Look at this saggy old fucker, Tony. What d'you reckon? What shall we do with him?"

"Put him down, Benny."

Benny shook his head from side to side, making a

tutting noise with his tongue.

"Tut. Tut. Tut," he said looking straight at me.

A couple of beats of silence followed. Then he started up again.

"What's in it for you, Tone? That's what I don't understand," he paused for a moment. "After everythin' I've done for you."

Then Benny turned back to face The Mole. He shoved his face about six inches in front of him.

"Look at him ... a greasy, nasty, toerag."

He tightened his grip on The Mole, then pulled his face even closer.

"My man Anif wants to have a little chat with you."

Then he whacked The Mole again, this time with his fist. I heard the crack of bones, and The Mole wobbled on his feet.

Benny shoved him onto the floor as he struggled to keep his balance. The Mole sprawled out as he hit the surface.

At that moment I dived across the room, shoved Jenny out of the way and tried to get hold of that gun under the pillow.

It wasn't there.

The Mole rolled over and tried to get up. A trickle of blood was coming from the corner of his mouth.

Jenny woke up looking confused and frightened and started screaming.

Benny said: "Now look what you've gone and done."

He paused and looked admiringly at Jenny.

"Sleepin' Beauty. You alright my little darlin'?"

Jenny blinked at least half a dozen times. She was having trouble working out where she was.

Then Benny said to Jimmy The Mole: "It's all your fault. You sick piece of shit. You made her like this. Not us."

The Mole was still on his knees, but I could see he was trying to open his brief case.

"She had no-one else to turn to but her Uncle Benny. She fuckin' hated you after what you did to her ..."

By now Jimmy The Mole was taking out his shooter. He raised it in both hands, aimed at Benny's chest and pulled the trigger.

The first shot drove Benny's head to the right. The second and third bullet hit as he slumped against the wall. Blood streaked the floral wallpaper. Benny, leaned on the wall as if he'd been nailed to it. Then he made a nasty croaking noise and his head slumped to one side.

"Fuckin' hurts don't it?" The Mole shouted at him.

But Benny wasn't listening. Still on his knees he pumped another bullet into Benny's body. But I reckon he was already dead.

"For fuck's sake!" I screamed. "Stop!"

Then the door smashed open, and Anif was there with his two clowns. He took in what was happening at a glance and started moving rapidy towards The Mole. He had one of his favourite razors in his hand.

The Mole was still yelling at Benny's punctured corpse.

"Fuckin' hurts, don't it?" he cried. He rocked back and forth as he said it. "Fuckin' hurts, don't it? Fuckin' hurts, don't it?"

Then he turned the shooter on Anif who looked at him with a nasty, smirking expression on his face.

"Come on, big man. You gon' ta blow me away?" Anif spat the words out with utter contempt.

His smirk had become the nastiest smile I'd ever seen in my life. The Mole put him out of his misery. He squeezed the trigger, and Anif spun violently in mid-stride, the blood exploding from his shattered chest. He collapsed in the doorway, twitching and dying.

Henry and Del were out the door before Anif's corpse hit the floor.

Jimmy The Mole straightened up, sweat ran down his face and blended with the blood seeping from his mouth. He held the shooter steady, both hands firmly on the stock, two fingers compressing the trigger past its safety point.

Jenny remained on the bed, sprawled face down, screeching and sobbing uncontrollably. The Mole turned towards me, the barrel pointed straight at me.

"Now it's your fuckin' turn," he said.

I can honestly say I didn't feel even a flicker of fear. Just pure hatred for this man after what Benny had said.

I looked straight into his eyes. I had nothing to lose.

"Come on, then." I didn't take my eyes off him for a millisecond. "Fuckin' shoot me, then."

I watched his forefinger getting redder and redder as he squeezed tightly on the trigger. The barrel itself was shaking slightly from side to side but it was still aimed in my face.

We stood there for a few seconds. My eyes snapped from his face to forefinger then back to his face. The barrel was rocking even more from side to side.

He stepped slightly back out of my reach.

"I'm gonna do you," he said.

I shook my head from side to side.

"Why?"

" 'Cos ...'Cos you're just the same as the rest of them."

"Maybe you're right," I said.

"I know I am."

I nodded.

Then my eyes panned over towards Benny's body and for a brief moment that distracted The Mole. The gun wobbled even more.

That was when I smacked him viciously around the head and ducked to one side just in case he let off a shot. I brought the heel of my hand down hard on his wrist and the gun crashed to the floor.

The Mole reeled around, and fell loosely against the side of the bed. He was shaking, but he made no sound.

I looked straight at him.

The Mole turned his head to face me. His eyes were dry and cold.

Just then those spotless white kid leather boxing gloves fell off Jenny's bed onto the floor.

I stepped over Anif's body, and went into the corridor. There was a group of people standing at the other end of the corridor, looking at the blood splattered across the walls.

I carried on walking, head down at a steady pace and ignoring all the gasps coming from the gawpers.

I went down the back stairs of the hotel and headed off down to the promenade, walking along in the sunshine, just another day tripper.

When I got to a set of concrete steps with ornate metal banisters I walked down them, and came to a lower level where dozens of badly painted timber changing huts had been built.

A girl was lying in front of one of them, sunbathing on a towel. She lay face down, her bikini top undone.

I crunched past her on the pebbled beach and stared out towards the sea. It was nearly midday, and the sun sparkled warmly across the slight ripples on the water. I felt sick, angry, frightened.

How the fuck had I managed to get myself in such a mess?

Along the promenade above I could hear police sirens, cars screeching. But it all seemed a million miles away. The noises didn't seem to relate to me. I heard one motor come to a halt on the road behind me.

People on the beach in front of me were looking behind me at the road and the hotel beyond. They were shading their eyes to get a better look. Even the girl on the towel sat up. She then put on her sunglasses and stood up.

Then finally I turned around. The Old Bill were up by the rail looking down towards me. I recognized a couple of people who'd been part of the crowd in the corridor. They were pointing me out. I didn't try to run. I just shrugged my shoulders, thrust my hands deep into my pockets and went slowly up towards them.

THE BOSS